"Marcus?" she sounds worried. I still cannot see her.

But then I can. As if someone has come along with a spotlight and *bang*, lighted Jules, and only Jules, for me. Only no, she is not being lighted. She *is* light. It is coming up from her. I cannot see my own hand, but Jules is luminous.

And she is so, so fine, so exquisite, that I try to speak but cannot. She doesn't even attempt to speak. In fact she looks as if she couldn't. She looks as if there is no life in her, like one of those perfectly preserved, suspended beauties under glass, under a spell. Sleeping Beauty with eyes wide open.

"Jules?" I manage to beg. "Jules?"

"Marcus?" I hear, but her lips don't even move.

I lower myself and cling to her, but she's not responding. I back off again to look.

And it isn't Jules.

It isn't Jules.

Witch Boy

Russell Moon

HarperTempest
An Imprint of HarperCollins Publishers

Library of Congress Catalog Card Number: 2001097468
ISBN 0-06-440795-0

 Produced by 17th Street Productions,
an Alloy, Inc. company
151 West 26th Street, New York, NY 10001

First HarperTempest edition, 2002

Visit us on the World Wide Web!
www.harperteen.com

PART

CHAPTER

1

I am looking at myself, in the reflection of the still water in one of the many here-today-gone-tomorrow pools that appear in the woods. My woods.

Hands and knees sink into the damp earth at the edge of the small pool as I crouch lower, lower and lower to examine myself more closely. My bluetick hound, Chuck, is hard on my shoulder, he and his reflection every bit as confused by me as I am.

The frayed tips of my long black hair contact the water, and I stop. The reflective me and the actual one meld, a sort of liquid hair frame boxing us in together, stuck with each other. For moments, I cannot move.

This is no Narcissus here. I am not loving what I'm seeing, and would in fact be the happiest guy if I looked down and saw something else, someone else. I keep checking, every day, as I pass every reflective surface.

But I always find this face. And I ask again, "Who in hell is this?"

By the time I look around, I have no idea where my dog is. They are familiar woods, our woods, and Chuck could be in any part of them. Something happens, I guess, when I go looking, when I go thinking, when I go down there into reverie. I don't know what it is, but it upsets Chuck, and he's gone.

"Chuck," I call out, and hear my voice roll out, around, and back to me. Birds alight, critters skitter, but Chuck does not return.

I know he hears me. I hate it when he does this. He's being dramatic. Either that or he's getting laid.

"Chuck!" I bellow.

He has no sense, no discretion, no discrimination. My dog feels about sex the way most cats feel about killing: anything that moves.

"Chuck!"

I surprise myself with the intensity of my yell. He makes me get like this. It's not that he has to be obedient and stupid all the time like other dogs. We don't have that kind of relationship. It's well beyond that. We're more like brothers. It's like if your younger brother were going around having loads of sex before you ever even . . .

"Chuuuuck!"

The entire woods shake with my rage. I squeeze my eyes shut, my fists pulled so tight my fingertips just might pop through the backs of my hands.

4

I open my eyes to see it actually happening, the trees trembling, pine needles and leaves parachuting to the ground, branches snapping.

One old maple, thirty yards ahead, finally gives up and falls with a cracking, snapping fanfare. Three younger trees are flattened underneath.

"Cool," I say, coolly. I used to scare myself when I did this kind of almighty crap. But you get used to it. What else can you do?

The dog yelps. He remains in hiding.

I am patient.

The tree quietly shifts, rustles, as if settling down into death. Only it's reversing. It comes up off the ground a foot, then three, then six, as if pushing itself up, then slaps back to earth.

I did that, you see. It's what I do.

The dog yelps again.

"I see a big boulder," I say out into the distance. "Chuck, would you like to see the big boulder?"

Chuck does not want to see the big boulder. He comes slinking out of the brush. He won't look at me as we resume our walk, to our place. First I scared him into the trees with my inexplicable behavior, then I scared him back out likewise.

This of course is totally unfair, but what isn't? It is not Chuck's fault that I am tense and frustrated. But it's not mine either.

"What was it this time, Chuck, you pervert? A chipmunk? A duck?"

It is not his fault, what is happening to me, to us. It is

not his fault that we are not what we once were. We are not a boy and his dog. Haven't been for about six months now, since around when I turned seventeen, and things have gotten weirder and weirder. Things like not recognizing my own reflection. Things like knocking down trees and throwing two-ton rocks. Without even touching them.

You know, things like that.

And that is the extent of what I know.

There is more to know. You know there's got to be more to know.

So who does know?

Maybe Chuck. My best friend, my better me. The further I get from myself, from knowing myself, the more I feel I need him by my side. I have no explanation for this, I simply feel it.

But if he does know, he's not talking.

"Sorry," I say to him as we reach our spot. I crouch down, run my hand lightly over his flat, velvety head and make sure his eyes catch mine. "Sorry," I say.

He snorts, then circles around behind me and climbs on my back. I climb us up the tree.

This is as close as we get, these days, to rightness. We are sitting in our tree, in our woods. Like we do. We are above it all, away from it all, yet somehow in control of it all.

When we're up here, I immediately feel a different relationship with everything. I look across the woods, the fields, the nearby houses, and on a good day, across the far hilltops. And if I can see it, it is mine.

Like I said, I move things. With my mind. The rocks, boulders, rotting tree trunks in the woods below us. Cows in the meadow beyond. I look at them, stare at them, think about them where they are and think about them someplace else. And there they go. Haven't you always wanted to do that? You have, of course. I always did, and then I did it. I stared at one of those big-headed cows, standing in the same spot, chewing the same plug of cud over and over, until I just couldn't take it anymore, and somewhere, way deep in the itchiest innermost section of my brain, some synapsey thing screamed, *Do something with yourself, you goddamn cow!* And then, before I could even comment to Chuck on the irony of it all, HowNow—that's what me and Chuck named her—HowNow was chewing from the farthest point away in the field. Just where I'd imagined throwing her in my frustration.

That's how I found out I could do it. I've thrown a lot of crap now, in the last six months.

It is the one single singular thing I do, and I haven't the vaguest idea how I do it. Chuck and I are the only two who know about it, because until I get a grip on whatever the hell is happening, I don't dare try to explain it to anyone else.

I'm afraid of what someone might say or do. I'm afraid of what I might say or do.

I'm afraid, to tell the truth, of being whatever the hell it is I am.

I look at Chuck whenever I've done *it*, and he gives me the look. Wrinkles up his intelligent, dirty sweat sock of a face in slow-eyed recognition. Appreciation. He's my dog, my boy. Whatever I do, he will give me the appreciation face. That's his job.

No matter what he really thinks.

"Sure, Chuck," I say today. "Big deal, isn't it? I can move rocks and cows. Does it do me one single ounce of good? Does it enhance the experience of being me one bit? I can defy nature, but can I throw a baseball two hundred miles an hour? No. Can I sing? No. Can I invent a computer games system that will bring Wall Street and Silicon Valley and girls to my feet? No. Trees fall down when I tell them to, and I'm still such a mouse in my own life that I'm jealous of my *dog*."

Chuck gives me the appreciation face. Superior sonofabitch.

"Right," I say. "Of course you're all serene and philosophical and all. I'd trade tricks with you in a second. C'mon, let's swap. You make stuff fly around, and I'll lick myself in mixed company. Whaddya say?"

Chuck knows. I know he knows.

He gives his boys a lick and grins at me.

It is a long walk home for Chuck and me, longer than usual. It is our last walk together in these woods, because tomorrow we are leaving Port Caledonia for a place called Blackwater. Nice college town: rolling hills, running water, good four-season climate with snow in winter and sweat in summer so you never wake up not knowing what month you're in. But more than missing Port Caledonia, and all the friends I didn't quite make here, and all the good times I almost had but didn't, I am going to miss bits. Bits like the big roundabout on the cul-de-sac where our house is. It's covered in crap from everybody walking their dogs there and not picking up after them, but we have the greenest grass and the earliest-blooming dogwoods as a result. I learned to ride my bike spinning around that roundabout alone four, five, six hundred laps at a go.

I'll miss the woods. I'll miss the woods badly. There are piney woods all over this part of the world, so I'm not afraid that I'll never find another one. But I will still miss this one. Things happened to me here. Me and Chuck became me and Chuck here. I learned to move things twenty times my size without touching them here. A guy doesn't forget stuff like that.

My dad shed the old mortal coil here in P.C. That is, he died here. Not that that should make much difference in how I feel, because I have no recollection of the man. His ashes were scattered here too, though I have no recollection of them, either. He was here and then he was not, and while that does not leave me with a bunch of memories of the two of us hauling catfish out of the river or throwing curveballs to each other across the front lawn, it leaves me with something all the same. It's not a memory. It's a memory of a memory, and it lives here.

I stopped being a kid here in the Port Caledonia woods. I don't know if that's a good thing or a bad thing, but I know it's a big thing.

I'm going to miss Jules, mostly. I don't even like to say it, because saying I'll miss her brings me that much closer to tomorrow and reality and being without her. She is my oldest friend, not really my girlfriend, really my true fine love. We have the kind of love, Jules and me, where we know instinctively that there has always been a sort of not-to-be-ness about us, but we are wrecked at the mention of being separate. So for the most part we've been leaving the whole issue alone.

Alone. Right.

Tomorrow is it, then. And tonight it's good-bye. We haven't even had sex yet, me and Jules—me and any-body—and so we have decided that we need to do it tonight. There's a party: we are meeting there, and when the music and beer and, I don't know, the lighting, are all right, we are going to slip away someplace and make love, me and Jules. Make love, me and Jules. That's what it will be, love. No matter how botched and weird and awkward the act is going to come off. It is going to be love. Making love, me and Jules.

I do like to say it.

Probably more than I want to do it.

I'm not a freak. Or maybe I am. I don't know what it is, but make no mistake—I am the problem. We would have done it a long time ago if I didn't keep coming up with strep throat and dead grandmothers and old weightlifting injuries. It is I who stand between me and *us*, because Jules is well into the idea for reasons not immediately apparent to any of her friends. I, like every other guy in Port Caledonia and a vast majority of the girls, would be honored to be Jules's bedmate or con-queror or supplicant or whatever the deal is supposed to be. Yet something, something deep and strident and genuine, has told me over and over: no.

But tonight I will ignore it. Tonight I will be with Jules because being with Jules is, even more so, too right to ignore. And then I'm going to tell her about what I can do.

And then, I'm hoping, maybe something will be different. And tomorrow we won't be as alone.

I walk into the house, the home, soon to be the memory. Right now all it is is a warehouse. Brown corrugated boxes line the entrance hall. All we own, save a few essentials, is in these boxes. The furniture, such as it is, is ours if we want it, but we don't. Nothing matches, nothing works, nothing much matters. Every stick has been picked up at a garage sale or a junkyard, and we couldn't care less. The new house comes furnished, and that was all we needed to know to leave all the old stuff behind.

I stop just inside the door and take in the reality of it. My life in a box. Every thing of consequence, of my life, of my mother's life, fits into pretty small boxes. If it can't fit into the bed of our pickup truck, it ceases to be part of our lives anymore. It becomes instant past.

I guess we live kind of blinkered. And that's just fine with me and Eleanor.

There are two machines that complete what you might call our family unit. One is clearly my mother's favorite. He is a green Apple iMac she calls Big Ben, and on whom she taps day and night.

"Hi, Ben," I say as I walk past the study/bedroom door. "Hi, Eleanor."

Eleanor is my mom. She is a very good mother and leaves me alone much of the time because I can be trusted and she knows that, and because I want to be left alone and she knows that. She is also a very good anthropologist because she never leaves her research alone. That's why she's got this big-deal fellowship. That's why Blackwater State College.

"Hi, Chuck," she says, looking up from the screen with a dirty, guilty smile. She always looks like I have seen her at something seriously intimate when I catch her alone with Ben. As if I'm bothered by her preference for technology over most human interaction. "Hi, Marcus Aurelius," she says.

Please, though. It is just Marcus. Birth-certificate-wise the Aurelius bit is true, but I don't use it. Would you?

The other machine is the one I shamelessly favor. Even Chuck gets jealous. It's Brainwave, and I love it and I excel at it. I check in on it every time I walk into the house, the way new parents must check on an infant. I enter my bedroom, walk to the desk, plunk down in front of it, and gently caress the thumbpads. "Yo, B.W., did you miss me?" I say as the machine heats up.

A groan comes out of Chuck. I disregard him. I am in position, poised, alert, good posture. I face the wall of my bedroom, where the screen flickers at me, on the opposite side of the wall where Eleanor's screen flickers at her. Like we are about to commence a gigantic game of Battleship.

12

Port Caledonia. Woods. Cows and trees and boulders and did I say I learned to ride my bike right out there on that roundabout? Six hundred circuits. Jules.

Chuck sighs and flattens himself like a rug.

The game begins.

"'Bye," I say out loud, to Eleanor and Chuck and this world where the rest of you dwell.

"'Bye," I hear in return.

2

The music is loud and uninteresting, and I can honestly say that I could not identify one single band if anybody asked me. Fortunately, no one is likely to ask me that or any other question at Doone Howe's party. Aside from wealth and good looks there isn't a lot bad you can say about Doone Howe. He was good enough to invite me to his end-of-summer party, which is commendable since I don't get a lot of invites and he doesn't know who I am. But there are a lot of rich, beautiful boys who still would exclude people just because they can.

And Doone has excluded nobody, as far as I can tell. I sit in the corner of his expansive living room farthest from the stereo, watching all of Port Caledonia's under-twenty-one population meander in. There is dancing going on, and drinking, and laughing, and head-butting. People spill out through the sliding glass doors and into the steam of Port Caledonia August, spread out on Doone's dad's pearly green lawn or continue out to the sand barge and even into the river.

I gaze out the window. You can forget sometimes, but from this vantage point the pull of the water, of the particular landscape of Port Caledonia, is undeniable. The clean, strong River Cal meets the estuary right out there, under the big bridge. Woods seem to accumulate from all over to meet here, hard by the running water. This is where forest meets ocean, estuary, river. Can't ask for much more out of a place than that.

I pull myself away from the window. I drink beer. And I watch. I am, for the moment, sad and mad at myself because I notice that this is also the kind of party where people could actually bring their dogs. I should get Chuck. Chuck would love this. Everybody is feeding pretzel sticks and tiny sausages to every dog who comes by, and I look at all the mellow mutts and I know if I'd brought Chuck that one of us would have gotten a little piece of action, at least. In the event the *other* one had chickened out.

I am a wreck already, thinking about Jules and Jules alone, and if I am any sweatier by the time she arrives I am going to have to tell her I went in the river with all the happening guys out there.

Which, I freely admit, I am not. A happening guy. I have never been what you would call an insider, couldn't even imagine it, frankly. But I'm no outsider either. Outsider has a certain something, a cachet, about it and, it has always seemed to me, a kind of b.s. about it. It's something to be achieved, outsiderhood, something you have to actually strive for, and I have just never been able to make the effort required.

So I am just this. Neither outside nor in. Just here, in a nether place. My natural place, and this suits me fine. I put a hand to my brow, and it is like my forehead is a melting Fudgesicle. I grab a napkin, walk to the circular Heineken mirror by the bar.

There he is again. Damn.

My green eye catches his green one, my gray his gray. The hand with the napkin sticks, welded to the cheek. My backbone trills, as I hang suspended in just that awful clammy moment between heating up and cooling down.

Okay, it's me, my reflection, but not me, not mine. It's off, it's altered, and it's changing, like it has been for the past months, since seventeen. It shakes me up anew, every time.

But it's better-looking than I thought I was, I'll say that. It has a certain something I never had before, undoubtedly.

This better not be puberty again, or I'll kill myself.

I am slapped on the back. I turn.

"Hey, ahhh . . . ," Doone says, pointing at me and snapping his fingers repeatedly.

"Marcus," I say.

"Sorry. Marcus, you having a good time? Can I get you something? A beer." He peers down into my paper cup, then runs off as if he has seen some atrocity down there. Then he is back with a new, frosty frothy one. Doone is a good host, a happy host.

16

"Thank you," I say. "And yes, I am having—"

"Cool, Mark. You keep it up," he says, then dashes off. He has a lot of people to be nice to.

I get a few hellos, a few heys, a few yos. The conversations don't go anywhere, and neither do I, for about an hour. I lean against the wall, listening to the music. I shuffle off to get the occasional beer, a glimpse out the doors over the sparkly river, a vain stretch to catch a breeze that's just not coming. Then I return to my spot, to wait.

Where is Jules? My Jules. My only. I would not be here if it were not for Jules, and I won't be much longer if she does not show. I would be just as happy, Jules aside, to be curled up in front of a good Brainwave right about now, Chuck at my feet and Eleanor on the other side of the wall, all of us coiling up and storing energy for what we have to do tomorrow.

"Dude," somebody says, slapping me across the stomach and passing along on his way.

I wish I had brought Chuck.

It's almost like the pull of a tide, the way a portion of the crowd is suddenly drawn to the front door as Jules makes her way through. Jules. What is she doing with me? That's me saying that now, but if you looked closely I am sure you could read it on every other pair of lips. It is loyalty, I think with great fear as I watch Jules's slender hands push outward through a sea of shoulders to make her way. She is loyal to me because of our time together, time when we were little amoebas splashing in our own little puddle, even now that one of us has evolved into a higher life form and one has remained me.

She is wearing a floor-length sarong thing of some gauzy turquoise flowered material, and an almost-see-through cottony white top. There is a hippie aspect to her, not in the haphazard way but the serious way they give you in the style section of the Sunday newspaper where it has taken a team of hundreds to get it that way. Only that isn't necessary here. She needs no help. She needs nothing. She is her own team.

But everyone wants to play for her.

The entire room swishes and sways with the wave of that skirt. Though the beer may be part of the swaying because the tables and striped wallpaper are doing it too. She made that skirt. My mother bought me my chinos and baby-blue T-shirt with a pocket.

"Hello, good-bye," she says right into my sorry, sorry ear. She kisses me on the neck.

I shudder, like a million tiny clawed hands are pulling at me, from my neck to my knees. Not good-bye. Not yet. I'm not steadied for good-bye yet.

"Whoa." Jules grabs both my arms. "Are you okay?"

I am not sure. I blacked out for an instant, and the blackness then broke as if it were a lacquered sheet of glass.

"I'm fine," I say. "I slipped."

"You didn't slip. You weren't even walking. Have you had, like, a ton to drink?"

"No," I say. I take a breath. "Love you, Jules."

"See," she says. "That's drink right there."

"Where were you? I've been waiting a long time. Missed you."

"You could mingle, you know, Marcus. It *is* a party. You could make friends, and then tell them you're leaving tomorrow."

Doone comes by, gives Jules a warm, knowing smile, which she returns. He hands me a beer, which she takes away.

"What was that?" I ask.

"What was what?" she asks before taking a sip of what should be my beer.

"That, with him? That was like, really *familiar* there, Jules."

She sighs loudly. "It's what people do, Marcus. It's called being friendly. It's called socializing. And you listen to me, you better start learning right now. I mean it, Marcus, I'm worried about you. You know, when I'm not . . . when we're not . . ."

All I can do is shake my head at her. I raise my hand to cover her mouth with two fingers resting as lightly on her lips as a butterfly on honeysuckle. Jules's scent is honeysuckle. But she was already done talking. She didn't want to finish the thought any more than I wanted her to, I know, and I only touched her lips for the touching.

I drop my hand, lean forward, and press my forehead to hers, closing my eyes.

"You'll do a lot more socializing when I'm gone," I say sadly, eyes closing ever tighter. "It'll be good for you, my leaving. It'll set you free."

Her turn. This is why we can never resolve anything. "Shhh," she says, and puts her hand to my lips. "Let's not

19

talk about it. Let's go upstairs. There's an available private space. In the attic."

My eyes spring open like window shades. "How do you know that?"

She giggles. Jules tends not to take serious matters seriously enough. Altogether too in control is her problem. If she could be more flustered, if she could be more fractured and scattered . . . then maybe I could permit myself to love her full on, guilt free. "I was invited," she says.

"You were?" I start scanning the crowd for suspects. They are all suspects.

She takes my face in her hands, refocuses me on her. "It doesn't matter, Marcus. We agreed to go. So let's."

Ouch. That is it. That is what I do not want to do, despite the inevitability of it. "I don't think I can. I don't think I can let you go."

"You're not letting me go. I'm letting you go, remember?"

It has become like having a twisted back, and no matter how you sit or stand or lie down, you can't escape the pain. The fact of tomorrow won't let go, no matter what Jules and I do tonight.

"It was Doone, right?" I say.

"It doesn't matter," she says.

"DooneDooneDoone," I intone, like a mad thing, like an angry toddler.

Just then there is a crash, an extended rumble, a scream that exceeds even the boom of the music. I turn to catch the end of a spectacular fall, our host coming to a raucous banging halt at the foot of the stairs.

He jumps to his feet, bellowing. "Who put the freakin' telephone table at the top of the stairs? Huh? Who's the funny guy who put the telephone table . . ."

I'm calmer all of a sudden.

"Let's take a walk," I say in Jules's ear.

"Let's go upstairs," she says.

I shake my head.

She growls. "Our last night. Is this it, Marcus? Is it not to be?"

I take her hand and start for the sliding doors. "It is to be. But it is not to be in here. It is to be out there." I point as we head out past the party folk, toward the river, to the woods beyond.

I pause at the keg and pull two beers on the way out.

"Love ya, Jules," I say, handing her her cup.

"We'll see," she says.

We have left the party house behind, then the party outdoors, then the river with high-school heroes splashing and drinking and dancing and smoking magically all at once. The music stays with us, the silly squeals and shouts and animal groans that sound, from a distance, almost nice.

"I have something I want to show you, Jules," I say, putting my arm around her shoulder and making an effort to fall into her step.

"Well," she says, "*that* is a romantic way of putting it." She shakes my arm off.

"No," I moan, "I don't mean that. I mean, I do want to show you that, too . . . but, no, I don't want you to *look* at it. . . ."

She smiles her toothy Jules smile. Too toothy actually, like she could be laughing at you all the time if you didn't know better.

I put my arm back over her and squeeze hard and serious, like I want to morph us into one shared body strolling the edge of the whispering river.

I feel a shock. It runs up that arm, the Jules arm, and comes to a stop with a bang in my rib cage. I stop walking.

"What?" she asks.

"I got, like, a shock," I say.

"Static electricity," she suggests.

I shake my head. "It felt like . . . I was painting the garage once and contacted an ungrounded floodlight. Buzzed my whole arm and gave me a chest pain. It was like that."

Jules looks concerned. I can feel her slightly withdrawing from my hold. This makes my heart hurt worse.

"My uncle describes his heart attack like that, Marcus," she says.

I pull her to me as tight as I can, and start us walking again. "Don't be crazy," I say. "It was just a little thing. It's gone now."

I'm not lying exactly. It *was* gone. But now it is back. Then gone again. Then back. For as long as I hold on to Jules this sensation pulsates, like someone is stalking me with a cattle prod.

To hell with them. I am not letting go.

"No heart attack then?" she asks gently.

"No," I say. "Love."

She nods. "Nerves," she corrects.

This is where I would normally let the matter go. This is where I can't anymore.

"No, Jules," I say. "This was my mistake, the letting-go thing. This is what changed, when I didn't notice. I don't love you like, the playground, you'll be a nice memory, thanks for being my friend, see you around, how's about a charity bonk for the road type of thing. I *love* you. As it turns out."

She stops short. I've really done it now. She won't even walk with me.

She turns to face me. Then she scowls.

"Well, as it turns out . . . ," she says, and gently head-butts me.

We remain stuck, our foreheads pressed together as if pasted that way.

"This wasn't supposed to be it," she says.

"I know. It wasn't it. *It* changed."

"Yes, *it* did."

"When did it change, Jules?"

"I don't know. A few months ago."

Bingo. I know now how real it is, because she is dead right. It changed in the last few months. Along with everything else.

But what does it matter?

"I'm not in your league, Jules. We both know it. You'll do better."

She takes a step back, then stamps on my toes. Her old attention-getter.

"I don't . . ."

"Would you wake up, Marcus? Have you even looked in the mirror lately?

"You're not the weedy little guy anymore. You've really—"

"Weedy?"

Actually I am not as surprised as I sound.

"Marcus," she says warmly, more warm than warmly even, as she pulls me by the hand, "you may not have noticed, but you have *arrived*. I always loved you, but lately I crave you."

Holy smokes, is all I can say. And I think I say it. "Holy smokes, Jules." Yes, there. Jules craves me. We're craving each other.

"What do we do about this now?" she asks.

"Now? I think *now* is pretty self-explanatory. We have now covered."

"So what about after now?" She even manages, for once, to sound unsure, to sound hopeful and nervous. If it's a gift, it's a lovely gift. If it's authentic, it's even better.

"I hadn't planned on an after now. I'd planned on good-bye."

"Think maybe we should dump that plan and try a new one?"

"Want to, Jules?"

"Want to, Marcus."

Holy smokes. Anything's possible. I now know anything's possible.

We walk along, getting closer, hugging all the way, through waves of confusion and joy and crippling jolts of real, physical pain. At least that's what *I'm* walking through. The sounds behind us shrink, the woods ahead grow. I have never taken Jules to my woods, even though they are practically my backyard. Amazing, even to me, but true. Why should I have never taken my one true only to my one true place? I don't know. Why didn't we ever have sex? Why didn't I ever ask her the simple and easy "will you be mine" kind of a thing rather than assuming she would never be? I don't know. Nobody knows what that barrier has been between me and Jules, between me and me, but I guess those barriers are falling, right now.

Now we're better, we're righted, and we're not going to let us ever slip away again, because I have my head on straight, finally.

For about a minute.

"We have to stop at my house," I blurt out.

"What?"

"My house. Come on, it's only a minute out of the way."

"Don't be ridiculous."

"Condoms! I have to get condoms."

"I have them," she says calmly. "You don't think I was going to leave it up to—"

"Sleeping bag. I need to get my sleeping bag. You know, pine needles. And snakes. You know how I hate snakes. I'll be petrified the whole time, you know that."

Jules sighs. "Yes, Marcus, I know all about your snake problem."

"And you know the woods here. Teeming. Even says it on the city limits sign, Port Caledonia, Snake Capital of the—"

"Promise me this is your last diversion," she says.

"My last, I swear." I lean forward and kiss Jules madly, and as I do, a thunderbolt cracks in my skull. I see a look of fright in her eyes as they catch mine.

"What?" she asks, disengaging.

"Love, again," I say, and lead her by the hand toward my house.

I don't know why I have to have him with me, but I know I do. I'm no kinkster or anything, like I want to do sexual stuff in front of my dog, but . . . I don't even know what. If I tried to explain it to Jules, I fear, I would seriously test our newly proclaimed bond.

Have I ever gone into the woods without him?

I scurry into the house, leaving Jules sitting on the steps, basking in thick misty moonlight.

"Hey, Ben; hey, Eleanor," I say as I pass their door.

"What are you doing home so soon?" she asks.

I am answering too quickly, too directly. "Party was boring. Too hot. Going for a walk with Jules instead."

By the time I have gone into my room, into the closet, into the packed box of my stuff and pulled out the sleeping bag, Eleanor and Chuck are standing in my doorway, faces demanding a little more elaboration.

"Going for a walk, Mom," I say, with a helpless shrug.

"Don't call me Mom at a time like this."

Chuck passes a loud blast of gas. Go, Chuck.

"It's just a walk, Eleanor."

"With your sleeping bag?"

I look at the roll under my arm.

"Just for sitting under the stars," I say, and with every

word I am curling inward, wanting to hide in the bag. "For protection. Pine needles. And you know about all the snakes—"

"I should . . . I should stop you, Marcus. I want to say you cannot go."

It may sound like I am supposed to supply a response of some kind in there. Not so. Eleanor offers me her face. I stand reading my mother's face. Reading the small flickers that register dead fathers and quirky anthropologist mothers and decisions made and not made because the origins of humankind are one thing but the here and now and sinew and heartbeat is another entirely. Forehead creases replay a scabby boy making six hundred lonely circuits of the rotary, and a face behind the glass watching, remote and loving, proud and powerless. She knows exactly how many friends and lovers I have had, as I know all of hers. A bountiful harvest it has not been.

We do not take things away from one another. She wants me to make the decision. I half want her to make it.

"You are smart, aren't you, Marcus? You don't make foolish decisions, do you?"

They are not questions really, but statements. Reassurances.

"I will be careful," I say.

She turns her back to me, pauses, then starts her retreat to her computer.

"Be careful," she says, as if it were her idea.

"I will be careful," I promise.

Eleanor is typing about three hundred words per minute as I pass her door. Eleanor is not a fast typist.

I step out onto the porch, and Jules is standing there, trying to be patient. "I was afraid you crawled up to hide in the attic or something," she says, slapping me on the arm playfully. Then she spies Chuck, popping out from behind my legs. He has that goofy breathy face on, like dogs do when they are hanging their head out the car window.

She slaps my arm again. Not playfully.

"He is *not* coming with us. Marcus—"

"Oh, come on, what harm could he—"

"Marcus," she snaps, with finality.

I stand rigid. There will be no Jules. There will be no proper good-bye, no fitting conclusion to our love story that deserves this and so much more, if I do not do the right thing here. I am terrified to go without him, though I know how insane that is.

"Come on, Chuck," Eleanor calls from behind the screen door.

Jules has a rare moment of bashfulness. "Hello, Eleanor," she says, taking my hand.

"Hello, Jules," Eleanor says warmly, quietly.

Chuck has taken advantage of the break to start slinking toward me again. Eleanor pushes the screen door open, sniffs. "Chucky," she says firmly. He hates that name.

Chuck takes a couple of tentative steps toward me. He feels it too. He needs to be with me out there. God, this is stupid, needing my dog with me the first time . . .

"Chuck," Eleanor snaps.

Finally he turns, walks toward her, looking over his shoulder every couple of steps. He skulks into the house, and Eleanor disappears like a vapor.

Jules starts pulling me away before I can prove my mother wrong by making a stupid decision.

"You have a great mom, Marcus, do you know that?"

"I do. Pretty good dog too."

Jules laughs. When Jules laughs I could cry. I could fall at her feet, I could dissolve into a pool of liquid, I could burst into flame. Even if I didn't mean to be funny. I am holding her hand as tightly as I can. Because I don't ever want to let her go.

"You know," I say, "one of the great things about Eleanor is she wants whatever makes me happy."

She matches my hand squeeze for squeeze.

"You make me happy," I say. "She'd let you come."

"And my folks," she says, oddly brightly, "would put up only token resistance."

I fairly jump. Even have to stop myself, as I feel the leg muscles twitch for a small hop. Now it's a celebration. That sounded like a deal finalized, there. Didn't it sound like a deal?

"Is that bag going to be big enough for both of us?" she asks.

A deal. With every stride now, we are deeper into a fabulous, fantastical place.

"Yup. It's a double. Used to let Chuck come in with me when we would camp out here."

She is laughing, again, even though I'm not joking, again. But I don't half notice. I am looking up, through blurry, teary, sweat-stippled eyes at the shimmery fairy-light sky. As we enter the woods.

Every step brings us farther into darkness. At first the

strong moon and spangly stars continue peeking through the branches, but steadily the woods grow denser. Eventually it is hard to see much of anything, and we navigate purely by my intimate knowledge of the place. It feels more and more like I have to tug on Jules to get her to stay with me. Not because of reluctance, but because of the blindness I ask her to follow me into.

"You okay?" I ask softly.

"Yeah," she says. "A little spooked, though."

"Not to worry. I won't let you put a foot wrong."

"Okay," she says, and I can tell she means it. She squeezes my hand a little harder, but she is pulling back less.

"I meant it, that I wanted to show you something out here, Jules." And I do, I do. This is it. The *truly* intimate act that I want to share with her. "Something you probably won't even believe after you've seen it."

"But I won't see it. I can't see anything out here."

"You'll be able to see, when I take you up a certain tree."

I feel her tugging a bit once again.

"How freaky is this all going to get, Marcus? I don't know if I want to . . ."

I pull her up close, and I stop. I can barely make out her face, though it is right in front of me. "Fairly freaky," I say. "But not like there's anything to worry about. You never have anything to worry about as long as you're with me, Jules. Never, ever."

I kiss her, both as softly as I can and as fully as I can. I stop, try to look at her, can't see much. I begin moving all around her face with my face, cheek brushing cheek, nose brushing lips, lips brushing eyes. Reading her features like Braille. I kiss her again. Then I kiss her again and by the third time she is kissing me back, and it would not matter what kind of lighting we had because my eyes feel like they are rolling back in my head.

"You can show me later," she whispers.

The sleeping bag is down, and I am kicking it flat with my feet while not letting go of Jules. I feel clothes, her airy fabrics, falling away a piece at a time, and I am squeezing her harder and harder, like I am holding on to life itself, life's own slim hips in my hands.

We are on our knees, and I am needing help. Help with a belt buckle, help with a twisted T-shirt, and I get help. We are in the sleeping bag, and it is pulled up tight around us, zippered safely against the snakes and the world, and whatever small spaces are not completely filled by down and polyester are filled by every bit of Jules and me.

I feel pain, but I figure you are supposed to feel pain. How would I know, and if I did know, what would I care? My head is hammering. All my joints are suddenly shot through with something like arthritis, slowing my movements, and punishing me for every one.

And every single one is worth it.

Jules gets softer. The parts of her I know so well, lovely as they are, lovely soft as they have always been, are nothing compared to the newness of her now. Her cheek, the underside of her chin, her neck I kiss a thousand times and will be back for a thousand more, but I cannot fathom, as I touch her breast, her belly, her back, how flesh so soft can hold together without melting. I close my eyes, open them again to feel the difference. I turn my head back and forth, to brush my lips over and over Jules's damp, honeyed navel.

I close my eyes once more and I freeze. I breathe into Jules. Her abdomen rises and falls gently, greeting me, withdrawing, greeting me. I turn my head, place my ear to her, and listen to the soft thump of my heart. I want every sense there is of Jules. Sound, taste and touch, scent and sight.

"What?" she says.

Startled, I raise my head, matted with sweat. I don't know how long I was there. Thirty seconds? Thirty minutes?

"I didn't say anything," I say, and make my way slowly back up to her face. I kiss every square inch of skin on my way.

"Oh," she says, sounding as fuzzy as me.

Her hands are on me, feeling me, and I am feeling me because of it. My ribs push out. My chest, under her hands, is tight, solid. Stomach muscles bang through the skin, pronounced and articulated. I have things I never had before, or never noticed. I feel hard, and very, very strong. Rivulets of sweat slalom down over me and make their way to Jules like streams to the bay.

I cannot make enough contact with her skin. My face, my lips, move over hers. My arms travel the length of her, my fingertips searching for any square inch of her where they have not touched. Our stomachs are flattened together, and for a time that is *all* I can feel, and all I need to feel. I cannot imagine beyond this.

Jules has my hair in her hands. Then she is on top of me. I still cannot see her, but the picture is clear. I am knowing her in the way I know the woods, which I could do without any eyes at all.

"What?" she breathes it more than speaks it. "No, don't say that."

We roll. I am on top of her now, her arms stretched out over her head, my fingers twined with hers. "I didn't say anything."

She doesn't get the chance to say anything else, as I descend for the longest, loveliest kiss that brings us, finally as far into each other as it is possible to get. We don't want to let it go, and for the longest time we don't. We lie there, mouth-to-mouth, motionless.

Then, suddenly, we are no longer motionless. Jules is biting my top lip. Then she is biting it hard. I groan. She is biting me very hard. I yank my head away.

I lift myself some, trying to get a look at her. "Jules?" I say.

"Marcus?" she sounds worried. I still cannot see her.

But then I can. As if someone has come along with a spotlight and *bang*, lighted Jules, and only Jules, for me. Only no, she is not being lighted. She *is* light. It is coming up from her. I cannot see my own hand, but Jules is luminous.

And she is so, so fine, so exquisite, that I try to speak but cannot. She doesn't even attempt to speak. In fact she looks as if she couldn't. She looks as if there is no life in her, like one of those perfectly preserved, suspended beauties under glass, under a spell. Sleeping Beauty with eyes wide open.

"Jules?" I manage to beg. "Jules?"

"Marcus?" I hear, but her lips don't even move.

I lower myself and cling to her, but she's not responding. I back off again to look.

And it isn't Jules.

It isn't Jules.

A desperate small moan-cry comes out of me, like I'm an animal caught in a trap, as I struggle, trying to get up, up off this *man* I am lying on. The arthritis has now seized me totally, and I am paralyzed.

"Marcus?" Jules's voice is calling me ever more desperately now; she is right here, but I cannot see her.

The man does nothing but stare at me, and then he takes my hands, twines our fingers just the way Jules and I had done. Feels like he's got a coating of warm motor oil on his hands, but it is blood. His hands, now my hands, are coated in blood.

I try to push off him, to get some distance, I am pushing him, shoving, banging, clawing him.

"Marcus!" Jules is screaming now, crying. I can only hear her. I have to get to her, I have to, but the man will not let me go.

He has got me now by the back of the neck, the back hairs, and he is pulling. He is powerful, much stronger than me, and I know I cannot hold him off for long. He is bringing my face down on him, digging into my neck with his nails.

For the first time I take in the face. I know this face. Who the hell is this?

"Marcus!"

The face is not a horror. It is sad and desperate and needy.

And I don't care.

I grab his hair with both of my hands, and I begin to hammer his head against the ground.

But he does not stop. His face, familiar face, pathetic, insistent creepy old face, waits while his overwhelming strength brings me down, down, down to him. I pull at his scalp with everything I have. He locks onto my eyes with his . . .

With his mismatched, green, gray eyes.

"Marcus!" Jules's voice calls, and everything freezes. Her voice is distant. More distant still as she calls once more, getting farther and farther away from me.

The lights go out.

Quick as it all came on, it is gone again. I am sitting upright and naked, and alone. Half inside, half outside the sleeping bag. I can't see anything.

"Jules?" I call softly, panting, wheezing.

No response.

Shit! I jump. I am bitten. There is a snake in the bag. I topple over, squirm around on the ground. Shit, I am bitten again, on the leg, and again, on the stomach, before I can roll outside the bag and then grab it by the neck, squeezing until it lets go of the soft flesh at my navel. Screaming, I throw the evil bitch as far as I can. I hear it thud, off in the distance.

I grab at the sleeping bag beneath me and find that it is drenched at the top, where our heads would have been. I dare not even imagine with what. I raise my hand to my face to wipe away sweat and whatever else is running into my eyes, and find strands of hair tangled in my fingers. I bring the hand close to my nose.

Honeysuckle.

I am stumbling, falling, banging into trees in these woods I know so well I don't need eyes. "Jules!" I call, and get no answer. "Jules, Jules," I keep calling.

I cannot imagine what's going on.

Was it a dream? Was *he* a dream? Is *this* a dream? Why am I here? Why is Jules not?

"Jules, Jules," I keep calling.

Was it the beer? Must be the beer. I shouldn't drink beer. I drank the beer and went home and crashed and got up and walked into the woods without knowing and . . .

"Jules, Jules."

Even a dream . . . even a dream . . . why such a dream? You gotta be melted in the head to even *dream* like this.

Where is Jules? Where is Jules? I am running so hard, harder with the thinking, I am banging like a pinball off trees. If this is all a dream, Jules should be here; if the dream is over, Jules should be here; whatever it is, Jules should be here, we were going to stay together. Have I lost my Jules, lost my bearings, lost my mind?

Sirens. Sirens of every kind are screaming in the distance. I vaguely wonder why before I catch the root of a tree with my unlaced shoe and hit the ground hard.

I am crying real tears as I get back to my feet and negotiate the last bits of trail out of my woods.

As I emerge into the moonlight, I stop dead in the middle of the road. The sirens are still blowing, and you can feel it, the action of the town. There is yelling, there is screaming, there is motion of every kind. There is no music, there is no party.

I have been dragging my sleeping bag behind me like a little lost boy with his blanket. I look at it now, reluctantly, and find what I did not want to find. It is blood. Soaked, as if the end had been in a blood vat. I look in my right hand, which is still clutching the hair. Jules's thick, chocolate-brown hair.

CHAPTER

I run. I run for home. I run flat out, the sleeping bag tangling in my legs until I sling the bloody mess over my shoulder and run harder, harder, crying, sweating in the sweltering sticky night, my shoes flopping, my belt dangling, my snakebites stinging, and my brain bouncing off the walls of my skull.

I hit the front porch running, then freeze.

On the other side of the screen door Chuck is planted, like a granite dog with suddenly green, fair, living, comprehending eyes. He is staring deep into me, knowing me unfairly. Like he shouldn't be. Like no creature should be knowing another.

"Stop it," I say.

He does not.

"What did I do, Chuck?" I whisper desperately. She was begging me to stop.

He stares at me, as if to burn something into me, for a few seconds more. Then his eyes go back, from this strange green to their usual murky brown. He backs away from the door. I am about to rush in; then I stop, jump off the side of the porch, and jam the sleeping bag into a small, Chuck-dug space under the latticework under the stairs. Then I go into the house.

I don't know what to expect. I don't know what I'll do. I suck it up and do what I do when I don't know what to do. I go to Eleanor's door.

Eleanor is gone. She is leaned all the way back in her multiposition orthopedic office chair, eyes tight, with the computer and a bottle of hearty Italian red singing her a lullaby. She sleeps there as often as she does in the bed.

At a loss, I turn and find Chuck. Chuck turns and heads for the bathroom. I follow, not because I think that he knows what to do, but because I cannot possibly decide for myself. Every step feels strange, every piece of floor foreign, like at any moment I will set a foot wrong and tumble through to someplace absolutely evil, someplace even worse than where I am.

I look in the bathroom mirror. . . .

I jump away, gasping. The face in the mirror is not mine. It's his.

If he's a dream, he's a goddamn potent dream.

I remain pinned to the cool tile wall. I close my eyes, open them, rub them. I look down and find Chuck still there, still with me, serene as Buddha. Slowly I approach the mirror.

I find me there. But it is scarcely relief that I feel.

Black sockets set in electric-white skin, blood freckles splashed diagonally from right temple to left cheek.

I fairly dive into the basin, scrubbing my face, hands, arms until I have probably removed the top three layers of skin. I touch lightly at the four puncture marks, angry red and weepy, around my belly button. They burn. If I'd had Chuck with me, that'd be one dead snake . . . I knew I should have . . . I knew. . . .

I look down, and Chuck is gone again. I panic, running from room to room to finally locate him lying on the striped cotton throw rug in front of my dresser.

I change quickly, hide the old bloodstained clothes in the packed-for-moving box in the closet, and follow Chuck, out of the room, down the hall, out the front door.

As the air hits my face it triggers my response. "Jules," I say meekly into the motionless wet atmosphere. "Jules?"

She does not answer, and Chuck does not wait. He is off. It's clear he knows where he is going from the start. All I can do is follow, and pray that where he leads is where I want to be. Where I will find my Jules, my sanity, and peace. Where I will find the explanation. Something in the universe owes me an explanation.

Chuck leads me to where the entire party has moved. To where the entire fire department and all the rescue services of the town have moved. We are on the banks of the river, beneath the town's one huge suspension bridge. The sirens have stopped crying, but the lights are all whirring away, throwing mad staccato psychedelia on the bridge, the water, and the dripping, mangled Hummer being hauled out of the fast-moving current (with some difficulty) by two tow trucks.

There's only one Humvee anywhere around here. And it belongs to Doone's family. It was sitting in the driveway when the party was on. Who took the Humvee?

I don't know how long I am frozen to the spot, but I am staring and immobilized even after I become aware that I want to be moving. Slowly, like a patient relearning how to walk, I lift and drop one foot after another, moving through the hysterical crowd.

Police are interviewing just about anybody who was at the party who can speak. And that's not a lot of people. The girls are sobbing, hugging each other, and the guys are making tighter and tighter circles among themselves, kicking at the ground, pacing off toward the water and then retreating to the safety of their numbers.

I, as usual, move through the scene like a spirit, all but unnoticed. Jules is not in the first or second or third cluster of girls I see. She is not with any of the silent packs of guys. She is not with a policeman; she is not in either of the two ambulances, which I half crawl into as I search for her.

"Come out of there please, sir," a paramedic says, taking a gentle but firm grip of my shirt. Once I am out I get gently nudged aside as the wail goes up, announcing the arrival of Doone Howe.

I am within three feet of the stretcher as Doone's bruised, puffy, beautiful face glides past me. He looks more like he's been on the losing end of a minor scuffle than the losing end of a hundred-foot drop. His mouth and the top of his head appear to be well bloodied, but he doesn't look mangled.

He also doesn't look very lifelike.

Police and medical guys are busy over him, pushing things into him, talking to him, rubbing his hands, arms, legs, trying to pull whatever bits of life are there at the center of him out into the rest of his body. The stretcher hits the tailgate of the waiting ambulance like a cannon-ball being shoved into a cannon, and before they can even get the doors completely closed, they are speeding off toward the hospital.

What the hell was he doing, driving out on the bridge during his own party? Did he go nuts too? Was it the beers? Was it something about the beers he was drinking and feeding me? I'd like to ask him. I'd like to talk to him. I'd like him to be alive.

Somebody is talking. I make like I need to restrain Chuck, and crouch down behind the cop who's taking details from Murphy, Doone's buddy. Chuck gives me an annoyed look, but I grip him harder.

"He might have . . . I guess . . . but he was fine. He could drive fine, officer. He maybe took a little some-thing, but . . . he was fine. We were out back, and then she comes running up, from over that way toward the woods. She was pretty upset, kinda babbling and looking all, like, disheveled . . . so Doone said he'd take her home. . . ."

Oh god. Oh god. What happened? What the hell happened? Where is Jules? She was running . . . from me? She was in the Hummer? Was she? Maybe he got her home first. Jesus god, he got her home first, didn't he?

Both Murphy and the cop turn around, spooked, as I topple over into the back of the officer's legs. I fall, right onto Chuck, onto both of them, as my world blackens again.

"You all right, son?" the police officer asks, lifting me by the elbow. "You okay? You want me to get you some help? I can call one of the—"

"I'm okay," I say, steadying myself with the help of Chuck, who's pressing hard against the side of my leg.

"You sure?" he asks, looking hard into my eyes from three inches away. He is probably doing this all over the place, trying to find out which of us are whacked from the party, and which of us might be able to help.

I look away. "I'm fine," I say, and as I turn I notice what I did not notice before. That here are two boats out farther downriver, with their noses pointed into the lazy current and spotlights trained on the rushing water. Divers bob to the surface and then disappear again.

They are searching for somebody else. They are trying to get her before the river dumps her into the ocean.

I can feel the policeman clutching at my shirt as I pull away, both hands covering my mouth as I dash for a roadside hedge.

"Kid," he says, then lets me go and do what seems the only thing to do.

Chuck sticks by me as I throw up, over and over again, into the hedges. I am on my hands and knees, and I cannot seem to stop and cannot seem to stop the rush of tears that fall off my face like I am some kind of twisted, demonic garden fountain.

When I finally catch some of my breath, I cough out a flurry of speech that tears at me even more than the vomiting.

"He was *rescuing* her, Chuck," I say, words without voice, words shaped by terror breath, by gasps. "He was saving her . . . from *me*. What did I do, what did I do, Chuck? Where is she, Chuck?"

Chuck tells me nothing. He sits like a normal dog sits, but he is staring into me like no normal dog could. I have inched up to him, to get as close as I can, and he refuses to either respond or to look away. He turns me back toward myself.

"Is this all me, Chuck? Am I responsible for this somehow?"

The lights of the vehicles are at his back. The natural light of night is in his face. Chuck freezes into a blue-granite dog.

I have to avert my eyes. I look at the ground.

"There's no sense to it, but I *feel* responsible. What did I do? What *can* I do? I can move things, right, big deal. I can move a rock, or a cow, or . . ."

Christ.

Or a car? If I went, like, completely psychotic, and Jules escaped in a Humvee with a beautiful rich boy . . . Did I move them? Did I *move* them? I look up and suddenly, violently, grab both of Chuck's floppy, velvety ears. "Did Jules get into his truck, and then I threw the two of them off the bridge?"

It appears, for all the worlds, surreal and otherwise, as if Chuck is unaware of my squeezing and pulling at his ears.

44

I am aware of it, though. I let go and stare at my hands. I am seized with the terror that I don't half control them anymore.

I grab two fistfuls of my own hair and pull as hard as possible, drawing myself face-first toward the ground. I can feel hairs coming out of my scalp.

An urgent sound tears into the settling sad quiet of the night. A car, up high, peels over the bridge, going about a hundred miles per hour toward the scene. It is Jules's parents' car. There is no way . . . no way can I be here to face them. . . .

Chuck rubs up against me deliberately as he walks past, back the way we came. I follow.

Nothing makes sense. Nothing is what it was. The ugly, rancid joke is on me, and somewhere there's got to be a blackhearted joker pulling the levers, because this is not me. I wouldn't hurt Jules. I wouldn't hurt anybody.

At least I am certain about Chuck. I believe in him, trust him. I need to trust him.

Because I apparently can't trust me.

I turn left at the intersection, and Chuck proceeds straight across it ahead of me.

What now? To the hospital to see Doone? Back to the water to join the divers and find my Jules and hold her and tell her how sorry I am for whatever it was I did? What, Marcus, What? "Chuck?"

He does not heed me.

"Chuck," I try again.

He stops briefly, regards me with all seriousness, then proceeds on his way toward home. He keeps on treading his serious path, but occasionally looks back at me over his shoulder, scowling.

"Should I go to the police, Chuck?" I ask as we walk. What would I even know to say? I couldn't confess if I wanted to, because I don't know what the hell happened.

The more I go on, the faster Chuck walks. I feel a desperate need to keep up with him, as if losing him means losing contact absolutely. Like if he ran too far ahead, I would get to the house and find there was no house, no Chuck, no Eleanor.

"I'll stop, Chuck, I swear." I am wheezing, and my eyes are blurring over again. "Just please wait."

Chuck slows, then walks at a leisurely pace. We keep it like that, keep it slow and quiet for the rest of the route. Like a couple of nursing-home escapees grown scared and cold, so they come creeping back to the home.

Eleanor is asleep, this time in her bed. The computer is off, and she breathes almost silently, the way she does. There are no ticking clocks, no buzzing electronic anythings, as we have packed just about everything to throw into the back of the pickup tomorrow.

I walk around the house. Hallway, kitchen, hallway, bedroom, hallway, living room, and all over again. Sticks of weathered, crappy furniture haunt the rooms, and boxes dominate the halls.

"Jules," I whisper.

If I don't understand anything anymore, then nothing has to make sense. "Jules," I whisper. If anything is possible now, then anything is possible.

But Jules is not here.

Is Jules anywhere?

I cannot sleep, no way, no how. I walk through the rooms one more time, like a dog doing circles before settling in front of the fire. Then I sit down in front of my last-to-be-packed necessity.

I power up Brainwave, start up Gaul, and commence fighting. The stick, as I grip it, squeeze it, toggle it around, feels substantial, real, right. I am in control. Everything before me does as it is supposed to, does as I say. Go right, go left. Thrust, Warrior. Jump, Messenger. I inch my chair closer. My face is three inches from the screen.

Chuck settles in on the floor next to me, and I lean harder and harder into my game of swords and sticks. I am good. I am great. I wonder if anyone anywhere is as good at this as I am and I think, *No, nobody is*. Which is only fair, since this is it for me. The only activity I can claim as mine aside from moving things. I cannot dance or run or hit a ball particularly well. I cannot win a debate, give a lecture, sing, or even speak to my peers without difficulty. We are shortchanged, I think, in some places, but compensated in others.

I live in here, in the game, the way I don't ever fully live out *there*. I have keys and joystick and thumbpad and rules here. It is probably where I belong. It is probably where I should have been tonight, instead of trying to be what I was not, do what I could and should not. I am not parties. I am not beer and songs and socializing, and I have known that for always.

And I am not Jules. No, I am Jules, totally, but in my

way. I should have left her alone. I should not have been the prince sweeping her up and off to my castle far away. Loving Jules is me, but loving her from a distance.

You shouldn't mess with things as they should be.

I am cutting off heads now, the way a florist trims stems for the masses on Valentine's Day. There is more blood than usual. There is loads of blood. Heads are popping off, rolling on the ground, turning to look at me. I cannot stop. I cannot stop chopping. Warrior is not Warrior. He is Marcus Aurelius, and he is rampaging. The game is making sounds it has never made, Marcus's feet making liquid squelch sounds as he wades through ankle-deep blood, exploding coconut noises as he continues to hack at skulls of people who are already well dead. I remove my hand from the controller, rub my tired eyes, then return to the screen to find Marcus is still at work without me. I move the stick to reverse him, but he doesn't heed me. He goes on slashing, chopping.

No. No, this is *precisely* what is not supposed to happen here. Not here. Not in Gaul, not in Brainwave. The controls are supposed to work here, all the time. The controls are supposed to work.

I turn to Chuck, who is well into snorty dog-sleep.

I look back at the game. There is a film of condensation on the screen. Marcus is grimly harvesting everything that moves. I frantically work the controls, but I have no effect. I reach and shut off the power, but again, it is as if I am not there, or as if the players in the game are real, and it is I who am the illusion.

All the victims have familiar faces now, but this does

not matter to Warrior/Marcus. He is killing everybody, mutilating everything he touches, until up comes Messenger. He pauses, pauses.

"Jules," I say, out loud. Messenger is my Jules. She stands, placid, eyes closed and hands folded across her chest. While every other character has been dressed in some sort of Middle Ages warrior garb, Jules is dressed in the same homemade hippie-girl outfit from the party. Only her hair is matted and extra dark, and she's all over . . . disheveled.

I, the offscreen, in-the-flesh I, have caught Warrior/Marcus's notice. He turns to me. He is walking my way, growing larger, larger, with his enormous sword raised. He is getting larger, closer . . . I pull back from the screen . . . he is coming through . . . his face, red and explosive, fills the entire screen. All I can do is wait. I no longer control that Marcus, and for the moment, not this one either. I am paralyzed.

A small cry, a whimper, comes from behind him, from Jules. He starts, mismatched eyes going wide as if he's being awakened from a trance. He looks at me once more, fails to recognize me, then turns away.

The bastard lets me live. *Makes* me live.

Jules too turns away from me. They are heading off, into the hills of Gaul, backs turned to me.

I am reaching out with one hand, stretching, yet getting no nearer to her. I am choked, with immovable sadness. I try to call out, but can barely croak, "It's a dream, Jules. What else could it be?"

"Marcus Aurelius," Eleanor says, gripping both of my shoulders.

I open my eyes. I have been playing blind all along—if I have been playing at all. I blink my eyes maybe a million times, and still there is a sort of film fogging them, but I can see the screen in front of me. I am shushing down the sheer face of a white mountain, skiing even in my state of unawares. Skiing in perfect, unblemished powder.

And in daylight. It is a new day. Greet the new day, Marcus.

I am still relatively motionless, gradually bringing all my being into play. I am moving only my eyeballs, like a cartoon owl, as Eleanor comes around from behind me and stands a safe few feet to my side, her hands folded in front of her.

"Hi," I say as if we are meeting for the first time.

"Hi," she says a little more familiarly. A little. "You get any sleep last night?"

I look around for Chuck, as if I can't make it through even this conversation without him.

"I put him out already," she says.

"Oh," I say, and go back to snowboarding.

"So?" she asks.

"Well, you just saw me, didn't you? Sleeping, I mean."

"In front of your screen? You call that sleeping?"

"You do it," I say.

"That's different," she is quick to point out. "What I do is . . . academic. It's research, it's work, it's our future."

I look up at her.

She sighs. "Should I make you breakfast?" she asks.

"I don't think I could eat, Eleanor, really."

She is being very careful with me, and I am getting scared.

50

Careful because I am giving off insanity like a musk? Careful because God knows what parts of last night she saw, heard, felt?

How much did she see, hear, feel? What does she know? What is there to know?

Maybe I never even went to any party. Maybe I Brainwaved all night. God, that would be wonderful, if I just Brainwaved. The game is so real . . . you can believe anything if you go too deep.

"I don't want to sound like I know everything," Eleanor says gently, "and in fact I don't *want* to know everything. But I know it's natural to feel the way you're feeling right now. There's a lot of stuff going on inside you right now, and you might not know how to react . . . but just trust me that it's normal, and that it will pass."

Normal? *Normal?*

"And even if you don't quite feel hungry, it is best that you try to eat a good breakfast. You are probably tired, a bit of a nervous wreck, and we have a long, hard day ahead."

All I can do is stare, gape-mouthed. I see out of the corner of my eye that my snowboarder is in the middle of an accident that will have him in the hospital if he survives.

If he survives.

"I won't bring it up anymore, Marcus, but if you want to talk . . . just know I am available." She stares at me, like I just did my first communion or something. Then her lip starts to quiver. "I'll make breakfast," she says, and leaves.

Oh. Oh, oh.

Sex. She thinks this is all about sex. Would it help either of us if I told her it was about insanity and spooky powers and maybe death?

I look back to the screen in front of me, and even Brainwave seems foreign to me now. Frightening. Slowly, like I'm with the bomb squad all of a sudden, I reach out, extend one finger, and press the Power button.

A blank screen. I have successfully turned it off. My heart is thrumming with this small sweet return to a basic.

I hear the back door open as Eleanor lets Chuck back in. He comes trotting around the corner, as he always does, and finds me. I am standing now, and joyful to see him.

He plunks himself down at my feet.

"Hey," I say, just as anyone would greet a best friend.

He wags his tail, looks at me blankly.

"Please," I say, stretching my knotted back muscles, touching my toes, holding my arms up as if to signal a touchdown. "Please, Chuck, knock off the dog impression, okay? I'm going to need you today."

He stops wagging his tail. Good. He gives me his old, appreciative, "you're my master and I love you no matter what heinous crap you've done" look.

"That's nice," I say, "but I need the other thing more. I need to know what to do."

Chuck's expression does not change. I brush past him and go to the kitchen.

It's French toast and bacon. I love this stuff, but I don't think I can do it. I stare.

"Can I have some coffee, Eleanor?" I ask.

She is already bringing it around, along with the bottle of Log Cabin maple syrup. She goes back and gets her own coffee, then sits across from me.

"Thanks," I say. I raise the steaming drink to my lips, am about to drink, then notice her milky, lost eyes over the top of my cup. I stop and offer a weak, unconvincing toast.

"To the new life," I say, mustering all the gusto I can, which is not a great deal of gusto.

"To the new life," she repeats, with a little more life.

We are still eyeballing each other as we sip. We are still eyeballing each other after we stop.

"All packed?" she finally asks.

"All but a few clothes and my machine," I say.

"Same here," she says.

I push food around on the plate, trying the trick of arrangement in lieu of consumption. It doesn't work if they're watching, though.

"Please try, at least," she says.

I try. I spear two cubes of French toast—yes, she has even cut them for me—and manage to get them into my mouth. Without any enthusiasm, without even the basic satisfaction of preserving life and limb by doing the minimum of feeding myself, I chew. The food, though it is as always perfectly done, feels and tastes like squared hunks of cold, live fish-flesh, with scales.

"You going to miss her?" Eleanor says softly.

The food is all but down my throat, and I stop. I try and cannot manage the last bit of effort it will take to swallow. I jump up from my chair, run to the bathroom, and spit up the toast and a lot more. I am in there for probably ten minutes, progressing from vomit to retching to panting to slumping. I roll to all fours, push myself up off the tiles, flush, and return to the kitchen.

She appears not to have even twitched. I sit across from her.

"Yes," I say in a hoarse whisper.

Eleanor leans forward, her coffee cup protectively between us though we are clearly approaching something deep and intimate. "I know I said I wouldn't pry—"

I hold up my hand between us. I have to stop her. I don't want to be rude—I love my mother to bits—but I don't want to talk to her. She is great to me, and I trust her completely, and we have a solid relationship. I haven't been able to tell her about my ability to move things, but I have always told her most everything else. If she is not there for me when I come home at the end of the day, then I get a little jumpy, but I don't want to talk to her. I want her *there*, but I don't want her to ask.

"I can't, Eleanor," I say.

"I guess," she says, shrinking back a little. "I guess I kind of figured. But I wanted to—"

"I appreciate it," I say.

I take my plate and set it on the floor in front of Chuck. He starts on the bacon and works quickly over the whole dish. Snuffling and slobbering, like a dog.

"I kind of wish your father were here right now," Eleanor says, as she starts cleaning off the table. Chuck and I both snap to attention. Eleanor does not bring up my father lightly, and never in any detail. "Well," she amends, "maybe not *your* father. But *a* father . . ."

★　　　★　　　★

It is an eerie, quiet morning as we load up to evacuate this life. I keep expecting the phone to ring, but it doesn't. I keep expecting something—I don't know, police, somebody, to come crashing through the door and give me what I deserve. To let me *know* what I deserve, at any rate. To put me out of my misery.

I would welcome that.

But it doesn't come. Nobody comes.

Maybe this is it. If I get out, if the hammer doesn't fall . . . then that means it never happened. Whatever it was. Maybe, if I make it over that bridge and out of this town, then that means it was after all, in a way, a dream. And Jules is all right.

"Jules," I say into my closet as I remove the last box.

She is all right. Somewhere.

All my stuff is in the truck.

"Now, Eleanor," I say forcefully, shocking her into submission. She backs away from the computer and watches as I disconnect everything and pack it up.

We're out of here. I don't even look out the window as Eleanor puts the truck in gear. I look down at my feet and pat my dog. Frantically, obsessively, beseechingly, I stroke his velvety self, over, over, over.

My leaving makes it all right. I should have left her alone in the first place. Should have left things alone.

She will be all right now.

I believe it. I have to believe it.

The other is unthinkable.

PART
TWO

CHAPTER

4

"**G**od, you must have been tired," Eleanor says, speaking to me through the truck window. I stare at her, look down at my feet where Chuck was but is no longer.

I remember nothing of the trip from Port Caledonia to Blackwater, because I saw nothing of the trip. I squeezed my eyes tightly shut as we approached the bridge out of town—squeezed out the sights, the thoughts, the world—and never managed to get them back open.

"Uh, yes, I guess I was tired."

"What do you think?" she asks, stepping back and making a broad gesture, like a game show babe revealing my prize.

Our new address. Eleanor saw the place once, when she came to finalize the job offer, but this is my first look. It is almost nightfall, so I have to focus to get it all in, but it is, in fact, a fairly fine house. The first thing I notice is that there are no other houses around it, which is a plus. Then there is a stream running loudly behind it, which is deadly cool. There is a large, bowing wrap-around porch that from the front appears to have no beginning or end, and only the one six-step flight of stairs to get to it. It is a smallish, two-story, light-shingled house with a gabled attic, and has to be at least eighty years old.

It seems utterly unimportant to me right now that the place seems to have all the structural integrity of a wet gingerbread house.

"Eleanor," I say, awestruck, "it's gorgeous."

"Yeah," she says breathlessly, "and surprisingly cheap. A previous fellow just gave it up."

"A previous fellow," I say, stepping down from the cab of the pickup. "Is that another way of saying a dead guy?"

"I suppose it could be. But in this case it just means the person who held the fellowship before me."

Eleanor and I are laughing, arm in arm up the over-grown stone path. It is as if the newness of it all, the rush of the water, the peace and clarity of the surroundings, have temporarily lifted from me the hanging gloom of what I did or did not do. But temporary all the same, I well know.

Then we hear the whimpering. We stop and turn to find that Chuck does not share our enthusiasm for the place. He is following, but at a crawl, and with his head hung low like a vulture's.

"Come on, you big baby," Eleanor says to him.

"Yeah, Chuck, what's up? Come on now."

He stops whimpering, walks marginally more enthusiastically. He has taken a bit of the fizz off the housewarming, because something's not right. I pause, I look, I feel for it, but I don't get it. "It's just a house, Chuck," I say. I hope I'm right, but he doesn't act up for nothing. He's Chuck.

The key is above the door frame where it is supposed to be, and in seconds we are inside.

The inside of the place revives my enthusiasm. We have always lived in decent enough places, but this house is *wow*, in an old Victorian, drippy magnolia, arches-and-groaning-floorboards kind of way. Decrepit magnificence.

We are immediately drawn to the French doors that open out onto the screened section of the back porch. I throw open the doors, and the flowing water announces itself as if it is going to come rushing right into the house. I cannot contain myself as I go out through the screened section and onto the open part. I lean right over, spying the cool rapids so close below you could drop a fishing line right from the porch.

"Oh," I say as the spongy, dead-wood railing caves with my weight and Eleanor has to grab me by the back of the shirt.

"We might be wise to proceed with a little bit of caution here," she says.

I nod but barely heed her. "Let's unpack," I say, and head right back out to the truck to begin unpacking.

I grab one of my closet boxes and march on, passing Eleanor on the way.

"Where's my room?" I say.

She is buoyant, the newness doing almost as much for her as for me. "Whatever room is yours, is yours," she says, laughing.

It makes sense to me. I will know when I get there.

I pass my scaredy dog lying on the porch, tell him to come, then go on without him when he won't.

Not now, Chuck, I'm thinking. *Can't we even have a chance here? Not now.* Right now it's all newness, right now.

I take the stairs two at a time, listen to the distinct croak of each one, then take in the hall view as I switch on the light. There are five doors. I walk slowly. Bedroom on right. Bathroom on left, bedroom on right. I stop, drop my box at my feet. I open the door straight ahead, pull the light string in front of me. Stairs. Steep stairs, and at the top, dark rafters under a hard-pitched roof. That, I think, could be very cool.

But not for *my* bedroom. I shut the door again. I select the last door on the left, and am instantly at home in the gold-painted, white-trimmed antique of a boxy room with two big windows, one closet, and one tall dark-oak dresser with oval mirror. I test out the bed, sitting down heavily, and find it gives way even more easily than the porch railing. It is so soft, it could be made of meringue.

The room smells musty, so I go to one of the windows and work hard to pry one old sash up from the heavily painted frame. The water splashes past right beneath my bedroom, and the sweet end-of-summer vapor swims up into my sinuses.

I lean on the window frame, close my eyes and breathe it all in.

"It is going to be fine," I say to myself. "It is all going to work out. Everyone will be okay."

I believe I believe it.

I turn and take the box to the closet. I pull open the sticky, swollen door.

And find the sleeping bag.

"Christ!" I snap and stumble backward from the closet, banging into the bed.

But there it is, bunched up in a mess of a ball.

I have become my own worst enemy, my own tormentor, haunting myself, jolting myself. That is a sleeping bag, like any sleeping bag, and I have to stop playing freak spook tricks on myself or I am going to wind up in an institution.

I go, slowly but surely, to the closet, to the bottom of the closet, to the bag. I hesitate, but just momentarily, then pick it up.

The head end is bloodied. Some of it is caked, some not yet dried.

I am too scared to even freak. I hold the thing in my hand, staring at it for a few seconds. Then I throw it across the room, smacking it against the wall.

Which is when the thick black snake slithers out, up the wall, and out the window.

Then I freak.

What the hell is happening? I think, as I run down the stairs. *Who is doing this to me? How is it even possible?* More and more, it seems this all has to be tied up together, in this one gigantic, grotesque joke. Nobody died, nobody's dead or lost or in a coma. They are all just laughing at me. One great, grand, final farewell present to me from Port Caledonia.

"What are you running for?" Eleanor asks, as she attempts to wrestle her unwieldy computer box in all by herself. She simply cannot wait for Big Ben. I take one side of the box as we head up the stairs. I am walking backward, but I can't help looking all over the place, like an antelope at a lion's watering hole.

We deposit the box in the first bedroom, which is as of this moment the office.

"You are a mess," Eleanor says, hands on hips as she looks me over. "You need a meal, and you need some rest."

"Not hungry," I say, looking all over the office for creepiness. I find none and head right back down the hall into "my" room.

I do not even look into the closet as I take the box I left there, and carry it across to my new, new bedroom.

It is nearly the same, only the windows—which I leave closed—look out over the expansive front yard rather than the stream; the bed is a single rather than a full; and the oak-framed mirror is rectangular. I catch a glimpse of myself as I head to the closet, then I back up. Eleanor is right: I do not look good. Even in the generously cloudy gray old mirror glass, I am pale and shattered-looking. Maybe it is lack of rest and food, and *only* lack of rest and food, that is troubling me. That stuff can make you crazy.

But those things can be remedied. And after that, everything else should follow.

I go about my task with renewed vigor. I grab the crystal doorknob of my new closet door.

And open it to find the sleeping bag.

A nap and a bowl of spaghetti Bolognese are not going to fix this.

There is nowhere to hide. I move my stuff back to the room I wanted, the original room over the water. I continue with the motions of unpacking the stuff, because bombed-out mechanical motion is all I can manage. But I can't manage it for long.

I make it to the bottom of the stairs before slumping into a heap on the last step. I put my head in my hands and cower. The little boy who thinks the world is gone, just because he can't see it.

"Marcus, what's wrong with you?"

It is Jules's voice.

I look up, trembling so that everything I see before me is swimming. But of course, Jules is not there.

I cower.

"Marcus, what is wrong with you?"

I don't look up this time. I uncover my eyes, but stare straight down at the knotty pine floor between my feet.

"I don't know," I say. My voice cracks. "But I'm sorry. I am so sorry."

"Don't get so upset, sweetie. It's okay." Her voice is sweetness itself. It is pure understanding, more than I deserve. But I must deserve it, because she is always right. I must be okay.

Her hands are on my shoulders. It's Eleanor.

She moves a hand to my forehead. "Are you sick, Marcus?"

I get right to my feet. *Eleanor*, I'm thinking, *I don't know what I am*. But I have to find out.

What I say is, "Is there a store nearby? I really need a Coke."

It is about two miles up the road. Chuck comes along without being asked, happy to get away from the house. When I hop out of the truck at the White Hen, he is right at my heels. When I get to the outside pay phone and start dialing with one very shaky finger, he lies across my feet to steady me.

I get through to the police in Port Caledonia.

I get through to the officer in charge.

"Evans here."

I freeze. It is all real now. It is so real.

"Hello. Can I help you?"

"Yes," I say tentatively.

"Yes?"

"I'm calling about an accident. A possible accident. That maybe might have happened last night. A car—"

"Who's calling, please?"

"Was there a car acci—?"

"Sir, who is this? Do you have some information for me about the accident?"

"So there was an accident."

"I can confirm there was an automobile accident last night, yes. Who are you?"

"Do I have to tell you that?"

He sighs an intimidating policeman's sigh down the phone. "No, you are not required to give me your name. Are you calling with information for us?"

I pause, a long pause. "I might be. I'm not sure."

"This is serious business. If there is anything you need to tell me—"

"I will. But can I ask . . ." I am nearly choking, asking the question, pulling the words, that I don't want but can no longer avoid. "Can I ask about the people in the car? Can I ask if—"

He is growing impatient with me, but he is keeping me on the line just the same. "I can confirm that there were two people in the car at the time of the accident. I can confirm that the driver is hospitalized, in critical condition. I can confirm that the passenger is missing, and that a search for that person is ongoing in and around the waters of Port Caledonia, but that the search has been officially downgraded from a rescue to a recovery. If you want any further details I am afraid you are going to have to provide—"

I hang up the phone, missing the hook twice before getting it right. I look down at Chuck, who certainly already knows. He is standing up now and leaning hard into my leg, and he leans harder when I tell him, "I did it, Chuck. Jules is gone, Chuck. I did it."

All the way back to the house, I can't decide. I can't decide whether to go back to Port Caledonia and attempt to confess the unconfessable, or to just snuff myself right here. I am deadly serious, thinking that these are the sum total of choices, as I pilot the truck down the road at fifteen miles per hour.

Chuck starts barking like a mad thing when we pull up to the house. Being trapped in the cab with the sound is overwhelming, ripping into my busy, cacophonous skull, but he won't stop, even when I shove him.

I kill the engine and tumble out of the truck, Chuck following close.

"Hello," a high, sweet voice calls to us from the porch.

It is too dark to make out details until I'm up close, so I push on, telling Chuck to shut up as I do.

"Oh, he's all right," she says brightly. "Welcome to Blackwater."

First I can't speak, then I can't breathe.

I fall to my knees, grab her around the legs, and hug as hard as I can.

"Jules," I say, moaning with joy and gratitude, "Jesus Christ, Jules . . ."

I notice that she is not responding. Not responding the way she should be responding, anyway. I look up. She smiles sweetly.

"Um, hello. My name is Eartha. You certainly are a friendly one."

"Marcus!" Eleanor gasps as she comes through the door. Next thing I know, her hands are on me, lifting me up off the ground. But I pay her very little attention.

Because that is my Jules. That is her long, thick, chocolate-brown hair. Those are her wide-set hazel eyes staring right through me now. Those are even Jules's clothes, even though I have never seen that particular seafoam-green cotton skirt or the yellow fuzzy top before. More important, they are *her*. Her handiwork, her style, her signature essential Julesiness.

I stare and stare and stare to make sure I am not crazy, and I am not crazy. That is Jules.

My voice is cracking. "I'm so glad to see you—"

"Very nice to meet you, too," she says, and extends a hand for me to shake.

I stare at it as if it were a lobster claw. What is she doing? If she is Jules—and she is, goddamnit—then she should be hugging me and talking to me and explaining what the hell happened back in Port Caledonia. If it is not Jules—in which case I am finally all the way out of my mind—she should be shrinking with fear over how I'm acting. She is doing neither.

"What are you playing at, Jules? *Nice to meet me.* This is enough now. I've been out of my wits, okay, with this. Whatever has been going on, it's over now, and I'm willing to get past it, but it's got to stop right *now*. Tell me about everything right *now*. Tell me what happened. Tell me, how's Doone?"

"What's a Doone?" she says evenly.

Too cool. Too cool. She knows what I'm talking about. Even if I'm insane, she knows what I'm talking about, I can tell.

"Doone *Howe*," I snap.

"Oh," she says, "it's like a knock-knock joke, right?"

I punch the air in frustration.

"Stop that," Eleanor growls in my ear. A man is walking up the path. "Stop acting crazy right this minute."

69

Then she reaches out her hand to the girl. "Hello, I'm Eleanor."

"I'm Eartha," the girl says.

Bloody hell. Eleanor doesn't see Jules. Is she crazy, or am I?

"Please forgive Marcus. He's had a very strenuous couple of days. I'm afraid I've left too much of the moving work for him. He needs a rest."

"I need Jules," I say to myself. At least I thought it was to myself.

Eleanor pinches me in the middle of my back. Chuck cannot stop sniffing the girl.

"Hello, hello," the man says robustly as he hits the porch.

"Dr. Spence," Eleanor says, smiling graciously while managing to throw me a look. "This is very nice, but you didn't have to greet us."

"Nonsense," he says, and hands her a bottle of ruby port.

This is the man who has hired my mother for the fellowship. He is about five nine, solidly built, and with this amazing, thick, shiny silver hair and a voice like a muffled trombone. You get the feeling right off that this is somehow the smartest person in the vicinity, somehow mentally bigger than the rest of us, even if he didn't have the heavy, Poindexter glasses, which he does.

"You've already met Eartha, my daughter," he says.

"We have," Eleanor says. "She's lovely."

"Yes, I've always thought so," I say, staring at the girl severely.

I get pinched again.

"Won't you come in, and we'll open this?" Eleanor proposes, pulling the door open and ushering them in.

"Really," Dr. Spence says, "we should leave you. . . ." But he is not leaving us, he is walking into the house.

Eleanor, who could not seem to locate one box a while ago, has homed in on the glasses within seconds, and suddenly we are all sitting in decrepit Adirondack chairs on what she is calling the veranda, sipping what looks and tastes to me like diluted Smucker's grape jelly.

My mother is telling her boss what a magnificent house she thinks this is, and thanking him for hooking us up with it. The girl—Eartha/Jules—is agreeing with her. I am doing a lot of staring, but I cannot help it. Chuck continues sniffing every bit of her he can press his nose to. The two of us are embarrassing Eleanor to death, but for God's sake, this is Jules. Life and death and Jules.

"Chucky," Eleanor says, reaching over and giving him a brisk slap across the head. He cowers and flattens to the floor. She throws me a look that says I am next.

I try and try and try to keep it together as the girl and her father tell us about the area, the school where I will be starting in a couple of days, and the social circle both Eleanor and I will just have to become part of.

I put aside the shudder I feel at completing any kind of circle at all and wait for my opportunity to lean closer to the girl. As she describes with relish the classic-movie house in town, I feign great interest and lean close to her, my nose coming within inches of her flowing, chocolate-brown hair.

Honeysuckle.

Damn right. Damn goddamn damnit right. She is here.

It brings a smile to my lips and mist to my eyes.

"Maybe it's time we should be going," Dr. Spence says, getting to his feet and motioning to the girl, Jules, to do likewise.

I look at Eleanor, who is staring at me so hard that if I were a snowman, I'd be melted.

"What?" I mime.

We walk as a group to the door and make all kinds of plans to show each other. Around, the countryside, the town, the ropes, the house, the way.

"So," Jules says to me, as the anthropologists study each other down the walk, "I'll be by, then."

"You'll . . . be by," I repeat. She sounds as if this is confirmation of a plan we have already agreed to. It is news to me.

She reaches out and touches me on the arm, looks me hard in the eyes, and I go weak everywhere I have any feeling at all. "I'll be by, then we'll get you caught up in a hurry. Cool with you?"

"Cool with me," I say firmly. She is going to get me caught up.

She seems so collected, so calm and confident, when she touches my arm it is like she shoots sedative through my veins. Telling me it will all be right soon enough.

Not soon enough. But at least now I have something to wait for. Something with Jules at the end of it. For this I can wait a while longer.

She leans forward, kisses me. Not on the cheek, not

quite on the lips, but just lightly on the corner of my mouth, where the lips come together and become cheek.

She is so Jules. She is so very my Jules.

Except the pain is gone. The tremors and terrors that more and more went along with loving Jules.

Vanished.

"Have you got an explanation?" Eleanor asks tentatively, like she's talking to a jumper.

I am standing in the entranceway of the house, at the foot of the stairs, absorbing this, guessing at which explanation she is looking for. If it's the *big* what's going on here, I'm as stumped as she is. I am hoping it's a little more manageable.

"What?" I ask, stalling.

"What do you mean 'what,' Marcus? The way you were staring . . . and smelling her. *Fur* was the only thing that separated you from *him*"—she is pointing at Chuck, who looks fairly embarrassed by the whole episode—"and when you actually took her hair in your *hand*, rubbing it between your fingers like you were buying bolts of fabric—"

"I never did that," I say.

"You did exactly that," she says.

Chuck emits a loud, snappy bark.

"Don't *you* start with me," she says to him.

For a minute we all stand there, staring, perspiring, waiting.

Once again, I am probably the person who should comment. Because once again, I seem to be the only one who was not in the room when I was performing these acts.

"Sorry," I say. "Whatever I did . . . sorry."

She sighs. "It's just . . . cripes, this is academia, Marcus. By tomorrow morning I'll already be famous as the mother of the kinky dog boy—"

"Sorry," I repeat. "Next time I'll hump Dr. Spence's leg if it'll smooth things over."

She sighs. She is not really angry, not really freaked, but perplexed. I need to help, I need to give her at least something to go on.

"El, listen. I think you were right, that exhaustion and stuff has really taken a toll. I'm not myself. I will be myself tomorrow, I promise. It's been a heady couple of days."

If she even knew the half of it.

I start up the stairs, toward my lovely, spooky new room.

Eleanor follows me, catches up and hugs me from behind.

"It has been," she says. "I keep forgetting, with all we have had to do . . . I forget . . . how it was. And it was only last night . . . of course you miss her."

I want to respond this time. I want to inform her how much bigger and weirder this is than she knows. I want to describe to her my feeling of suddenly being this tiny speck at the very epicenter of a profoundly dark and demonic universe. But a radiant speck, one that cannot hide in any corner of that universe.

I want to tell her how I am either the perpetrator of absolute evil, or the victim of it.

But I don't know which one I am, so I'll just have to get back to her on that.

And all this time she thinks it's all about my lost virginity. Which may just as easily still be with me for all I can figure.

"Thanks for understanding, Eleanor," I say.

Chuck has conceded and has come into the house, but he draws the line at coming upstairs. I leave Eleanor at her door, where she will comfortably and peacefully lay herself on the bed and take her rest among all the untouched boxes. I wish I could do that.

I go down the hall, toward the darkened rooms.

Darkened, save one. The attic door is open. The light is on.

I can feel my heart begin to pound harder. I worry anew about what it all means. Is there no end? Do I merely remain the plaything, the speck suspended in this until whoever is in charge decides to release me? Is the great cosmic cat nearly finished pawing at me, ready, finally, to bite off my head?

I stand. It may be thirty seconds, it may be ninety minutes. I exist, during this duration, only as a frame to hold up two hot-wired eyeballs trained on a spot at the top of those steep stairs.

I am supposed to go up there. I feel it as surely as if a great twisted hand were pulling me by the entrails up those dusty old stairs. Somebody, something, wants me up there.

No way in hell am I going. Couldn't if I wanted to. I feel as if I just ate a live, beating heart, and it is stuck halfway down my throat.

Eventually I manage to shut the dry, mewing door. Even that movement feels like a mighty act.

"Eleanor," I say softly. I am standing in the doorway of her room. It is dark enough to see shapes and not details. The screenless window is open a few inches, and the lacy curtain hangs defiant, motionless in the face of the powerless night air.

"Eleanor," I say, still sort of softly, but not really. "Are you sleeping?"

She stirs. I can see her up on her elbows, head tilted incredulously.

"If I say yes, will you believe me?"

"Ah, listen, I was . . . I don't want to seem any weirder than I probably already do . . . so if you think it's awful just say so, but . . . I'm a little uncomfortable just now—"

"Come on in," she says casually, throwing down the other side of the covers.

I sit there for a minute, staring out the window. "It's just . . . my rooms are kind of acting up," I say, figuring this is the moment to finally let the guard down and give her a hint.

"Oh yeah," she says, her voice already almost asleep. "I know that feeling."

CHAPTER

5

The first few days in the new house pass, if not normally, at least quietly. Eleanor is very good about it. Tolerant, patient, motherly. The second night, and again on the third, when the day is at an end and we go upstairs, we say good night to each other as if it is just another night, and I am just another teenage guy big and bold enough to sleep in his own room. But both nights I reach the end of the hall to find the attic door wide open and waiting.

I quickly shop out of my still-packed boxes, and I retrieve pajamas, tank tops, running shorts, whatever is closest at hand off the top of one of them. I change quickly and return to my mother's room.

She is, as I say, tolerant. Or afraid to say no. But she lets me have this much and does not protest until Chuck gets wind of the goings-on and tries to share the wealth by scooting up onto her bed.

"No," Eleanor states on the third night. "This is where we draw the line. Chuck, go."

He is crouchy and whipped-looking as he slithers off. He gives me a desperate parting look, and I am almost moved until I think, *No, none of us would be in this pathetic scene if you had the balls to come sleep in my room like a decent dog.* He senses this, and rightly hangs his head.

"And Marcus," Eleanor says in the kindest tone possible. "This goes for you too. Tonight, okay, but this is the end of it. It is kind of unbelievable, after all . . . I could see how unsettled you were when we got here, but after all—"

"I know," I say, fully prepared. I never expected it to last even this long. "Tomorrow."

"Yes," she agrees.

Tomorrow it is. It is something else, tomorrow. My first day of school.

"Hello?"

I can only faintly hear it. It may well be a dream. If I were going to dream, this would be it.

"Hello?" Jules's voice calls me. "Hello, Marcus?"

I am absorbing it, loving it, rolling in it. I turn over, open my eyes.

"Oh," I snap, sitting upright in bed and pulling the sheet up over my chest. "Oh, Jules, sorry—"

"No, *I'm* sorry," she says.

"Oh," Eleanor gasps, "oh, my . . ."

She backs out into the hallway. "I'm so sorry. The front door was wide open. And I called and called, and then the dog led me. . . ."

Eleanor and I both stare at Chuck, who is sitting in the doorway like a stone lion guarding a palace.

"Didn't you close the front door last night?" Eleanor asks.

"I did." I did, I am certain.

"I am sorry. I came a little early . . . to show you around school, introduce you around—"

"School!" I say. "Listen, ah, could you meet me downstairs? I'll just be a second."

"Sure," she chirps.

When I hear her descend the steps, I stumble out of bed. I am choking, imagining what she is thinking. If I wasn't already winning the freak-of-the-week award, this was going to seal it.

"Jesus" is Eleanor's take on the situation. "The dog-boy thing is going to be *nothing*, next to this."

I grab Chuck by the scruff of the neck and drag him down the hall with me. I sling him into my bedroom and make him stay there while I dress. "Get used to it," I say. "Because this is where you and I are sleeping, tonight and from now on."

I must take my time. So many of my instincts have been wrong. I can fairly well rely on the fact that, whatever thoughts I have about how to proceed, those thoughts are probably ass-backward. So I have to be cool, despite the obvious questions. How can it all be? How can any of it be? How can I be walking here, now, with Jules? How can Jules be here and be calling herself Eartha and getting away with it? How can she be here *and* in the bay *and* in Brainwave?

This is it, you see. The problem. If I can't avoid coming unglued, there is no hope. And in order for me to hold it together, I have to believe this:

She can call herself Eartha or Luna or Jack the Ripper if she wants to.

She is really my Jules.

We are walking along the charming back roads between the house and school, chatting about the local flora and fauna, avoiding any meaningful conversation or much eye contact. I am instead drawn for the first time to our surroundings. There is a sleepy, almost southern quality to the place, even though we are only about seven hours south of Port Caledonia and twice that far from the Mason-Dixon line. But the place feels foreign to me in a way I had not expected. Is it hotter? Are the trees dipping their branches just a little further down into the water from the banks of the stream? Maybe it's that Blackwater is a little farther inland, that makes everything feel warmer, soupier, slower than in P.C. In both places the water is the thing. But the water of Blackwater seems a lot less in a hurry.

The school building is coming into view before I manage to bring up either of the massive issues. We have meandered our way, along bank, out onto pavement, back through unkept fields of chin-high wheatgrass, and back onto the paved, settled grid of streets, and every change of scenery has been another excuse to talk about nothing. From the air the town must look like a patchwork quilt.

But it must be done, so I come out with it.

"That wasn't what you probably thought it was," I say, gesturing back in the direction of my house, which is actually about four changes of direction away now.

She will not let me off easily. "What wasn't what I thought it was?"

"You know," I say, my embarrassment deepening. "The, ah, sleeping arrangement."

"Hey, don't worry about it," she says.

"I *will* worry about it. I *am* worried about it. Very worried about what you think."

If this is what people in Blackwater are all like, Eleanor need not be worried about whatever impression I'm going to make. The girl is unimpressed with my kinks. She takes my hand, barely looks at me as she leads on, and enlightens me.

"Whatever you do is cool by me. You're going to find, Marcus, that we are some fairly free thinkers in my circle. Oh, I've seen loads stranger stuff than you sleeping with your mom. Loads and loads."

"Loads? And loads? I don't . . . wait, I was not sleeping with her. It's just . . . well, the house has been really creepy, and some freaky stuff has been happening to me. . . ."

She stops, stands squarely in front of me, and puts a cool hand to my cheek. "I know," she says sympathetically.

I am held there. Unable to move, unable to speak. Literally. It is like one of those scary nightmares where you are half aware, frightened completely out of your skull, and you are trying desperately, vainly, to wake up. But you cannot shake yourself, and you cannot scream.

Until, then, her hand is down, and I am released.

The first thing I do with my new freedom is, I shudder. The second thing I do is blurt out the Other Thing.

"You *do* know, Jules. So why don't you tell me what's going on?"

"Eartha," she says ultracalmly.

"So why do you look *exactly*, I mean, *exactly*"—I lean over and sniff her hair again—"like my Jules? Why are you doing this to me? I loved you . . . *love* you, and you know it. You loved me. What *happened*?"

At this moment, something happens to her. A softening, a saddening.

"I'm sorry, Marcus," she says. "Honestly, I am sorry about all this."

Frustrating as it is, unenlightening as it is, it is something. It feels like something.

But then she starts quick-walking away from me, toward the school building.

"What, that's it? That's all you are going to say?"

She stops, whirls around to face me, and, with a sweet smile, walks back, then lands a hard and deep full-on kiss on me. This lasts ten or so seconds, and I am nothing but hers the whole time. I wish I could stay here forever and ever, and never once open my eyes or ears to anything else again.

"No, Marcus," she says when it's finished. "There is a lot more. Trust me for now that I am going to get you through it. But a step at a time."

Even if I had a choice—which I don't think I do— I would trust her now. I was lost in her once she kissed me.

"But Jules—"

"And start by calling me Eartha. You are in Blackwater, and I am Eartha."

"Okay," I say, grabbing her arm as she starts off again. "I'll be patient, and I'll trust you. But you can answer me this one for starters. Am I crazy because I think you are Jules? Or are you crazy because you think you are not?"

She squeezes my hand and pulls me along quickly, like we are about to hit the scariest part of the scariest-ever roller coaster.

"Neither one of us is crazy, Marcus. That would be way too easy."

We have reached the parking lot. There is a lot of buzz. This is a much bigger place than Port Caledonia, a much bigger high school, even a much bigger parking lot. The lot abuts the school's impressive football field, and they are both the same size. Most of the students seem to have cars.

The school building itself looks like a long, low, sprawling concrete Wonder Bread factory.

"Earth!" Three guys together yell from a top-down red Mustang. There is no way they are not football starters. You can smell it.

It is immediately apparent that Eartha is wildly popular. Not a single student fails to acknowledge her, no matter how rushed they are, no matter how much first-day-of-school hubbub there is. She waves greetings more like a queen than a regular returning junior. And I notice that I am noticed. Some people just look, some nod or give a tentative half wave, but several I catch checking me out. They look at me from funny angles, then snap away when I see them.

One large, adult-looking student whizzes by before I can even get a proper look.

"This him?" the guy asks, then pretty much vanishes when Eartha shoves him.

"A new guy never arrives in this place without warning," she shrugs.

I get a small kick out of this. "You've all been warned about me, huh?"

"Oh, yes," she says, holding the front door open for me.

She says it so convincingly, in a voice deeper than her regular voice.

A voice that's not Jules's voice.

I shiver.

The entire morning is spent getting class assignments. Mostly it is filling out forms, waiting in lines, having thirty-second conferences with teachers, coaches, and guidance counselors, then standing in some more lines. It is a very up-to-date school, so every time I make a decision—yes, I think I will take third-year Spanish; no, thanks anyway but debate club, tempting as it sounds, is not for me; I'd prefer study hall to typing—I have a new computer printout in my hands within seconds. The system is so responsive to my thoughts, I half expect my lunch selections to be waiting for me in the cafeteria.

As arranged, Eartha meets me in the caf at twelve forty-five. I am seated, waiting for her, when she comes up to me.

"I pulled you a tray," she says. "Hope you don't mind. Lasagna, garlic bread, chocolate milk."

I am staring at it. "No, not at all. This is all great."

When I look up again, the contents of the plate no longer matter. I won't be able to eat them.

"Oh, Marcus," Eartha says, "this is Arj. Arj, this is Marcus."

"Yo, Marcus. Welcome," Arj says.

He is Doone Howe. Unfairly handsome, blond, tidy Doone. Doone's six-foot, point-guard build. Doone's cheery smile.

"Doone," I say in a choked voice.

"Arj," he repeats, still friendly. He takes the seat across from me. I can only imagine how I must seem to these people. I feel like I'm being strangled and thumped in the chest at the same time.

"You're doing it again," Eartha says wearily, "that thing where you call people names other than what they tell you to call them."

I nod. Where she leads, I will follow. For now.

"Been hearing quite a bit about you," Arj says.

"Really?" I am staring.

"What are you staring at?" Eartha asks, slicing her very firm lasagna into tidy little triangles. I look up at her.

"Nothing," I say, and begin staring at her. She chews, just as Jules did, *does*, with neat, mannerly precision. Her jaws hardly seem to separate enough for her to masticate, and she dabs her full lips with a napkin after each and every bite.

"Yes, you were staring, Marcus, and now you are doing it to me. Flashbacks again?"

"He has flashbacks?" Arj asks. He sounds very concerned. Why should he sound very concerned? He just met me. I wouldn't care if I heard *he* was having flashbacks.

"This is it," I say coolly to Eartha. "You guys are gassing me somehow. It has to stop. All right, maybe I did something, back there, in the woods. . . ." I turn to Arj. "But it was *your* fault if I did, because it was *your* party, and if . . ."

Just then, it comes to me strong. I snap up out of my chair. "You did it, right? Right, right, you're the one who kept feeding me the beers . . . stupid me. There I was, after my whole life in Port Caledonia thinking, duh, what a coincidence, people start being friendly to me the very night before I leave. What an idiot. Nobody is that nice. What was I thinking? You sadistic monsters." I make the effort to pan over the two of them equally, looking from one to the other and back again. I don't know how or why Jules would be involved, but how could she not be? The thought makes my heart hurt. "You'd been working on this for ages, hadn't you?"

I stare down at them with malevolence, and triumph. I have rooted them out. Maybe. Partly.

From their blank expressions, it would seem they feel otherwise.

"He's been having some readjustment problems," Eartha says to Arj. Like two consulting physicians. Arj nods at her. Then he addresses me.

"Please sit down," he says kindly.

I resist. I am defiant. I look out across the cafeteria to find that I am attracting no small amount of attention, and this worries me tremendously. I am torn between my need to resist and my need to be unnoticed.

There is a hand on my arm now, and the issue is over before I can even deliberate. Eartha's touch has caused my knees to bend involuntarily, and I am lowering myself into my seat as I stare into her wide, wondrous eyes.

"Jules," I say imploringly.

"Eartha," she says evenly, making a chopping motion on the table between us.

I turn to Arj. "Doone," I say.

"Arj," he says, smiling.

"So then why are you people so *patient* with me, if you think you're somebody but I think you're somebody else?" I ask.

"He asks a good question," Arj says.

Eartha nods, but then goes back to eating.

"Can I have a look at that?" Arj asks, indicating my course schedule. I hand it over.

"And eat your lunch," Eartha says. "You'll never get any better if you don't eat."

"Better? Am I sick? Is that it?"

"No. But you are weakened. And you'll need to be strong."

"What exactly will I need to be strong for?"

"Cool," Arj says. He has been staring at my printout and his own, hard, like he is trying to burn them up with his stare. Then he takes Eartha's schedule and likewise stares it silly.

"This is just great. We all have exactly the same schedule. What do you know?"

"What do you know?" I echo. The difference is, when I ask "What do you know?" I want someone to answer me.

"Fair enough," Arj says, and Eartha agrees. He hands us back our schedules. "We do need to talk. It's been kind of unfair, the way you were just plunked into the middle of all this."

"Yeah," I say righteously. Then, "The middle of all what?"

"We'll bring you up to speed on everything this afternoon at the Key Club meeting."

"Ah, after-school activities? No. Key Club meeting? Sorry, I'm not in any Key Club."

"Sure you are," Eartha says, pointing at the bottom of my schedule. "Says so right there in black and white; you're all signed up."

And so I am. I stare at my schedule, the schedule that I labored over all morning. It shows classes and a club I never asked for. What the hell is a Key Club, anyway?

Fine, I'll go. The wheel is obviously turning, and I can't jump off.

"Okay," I say, leaning right close to her. "But I'm going to find out, aren't I, *Jules*? I'm going to finally find out."

We are almost forehead-to-forehead.

"You know, you have the most deadly cool eyes," she says.

After school, when I enter the basement room that is the Key Club office, I feel like the temperature has dropped twenty degrees. Until I offhandedly mention this fact, and the temperature jumps twenty degrees.

"That better?" Eartha says calmly.

Better. Hmm. Would I rather be a little chilly, or control the weather? I get a trill of chill anyway.

"Better," I say. "Thanks." Thanks for what, I'm not sure.

They are lined up, neatly and respectfully, to be introduced to me. I shake hands as I am introduced to the core management of the club, called the Council of Youngers. In addition to Eartha and Arj, there is Marthe, with both skin and hair the same caramel color, who offers her hand like I'm supposed to kiss it ("A pleasure to finally get to meet you"); Baron, who squeezes real hard and does not shake ("That's my chair you're sitting in—everyone knows the green chair is mine"); and chunky, squint-eyed Winston, who takes my hand in both of his and shakes so vigorously and so long he almost does Baron's work of jerking me out of the seat ("Comrade, brother . . ."). It is all very orderly and orchestrated and has the feel of a coronation or a papal audience. Key Clubbers outside the Council mill about, playing games with ridiculous oversized decks of cards, drinking Cokes, and periodically bursting into spontaneous huddles, doing something you cannot make out unless you are in the huddle with them.

After the meet-and-greet, Arj and Eartha come up to me as I sit in Baron's green chair.

"I suppose you're wondering . . . ," she says.

"What does she mean, *finally* meet me? How long has she been waiting?"

"Don't be so modest," Arj says. "You're the event of the season, man."

There's that chill again. "I wish you wouldn't say stuff like that. No kidding. I don't want to be an event. Of any season. I just want to be a guy. Just a regular, like, junior."

Arj laughs, a warm, big laugh, like it's not at my expense, even if it probably is. He claps me on the shoulder and says, "Sorry, but there ain't no regular juniors in *this* group, junior." He waves his arm over the gathering.

I stare at them dubiously. Nobody, really, is doing anything special in the great and special group. What the hell *is* this great and special group, and why?

"Group?" I ask.

"Yes," Arj says, nodding agreeably. "Group. Our group, your group. Team, if you will."

"Team," Eartha repeats.

They are clearly having trouble with this very simple definition. I'm sorry I got the whole thing started.

"Family," Arj says, warming to the subject. He seems happy with "family."

"I already have a family," I say.

Eartha is out of patience. "Arj, it's been a long trip for him already, you know? Let's skip the *semantics* and—"

"In time," he answers smoothly, but with an edge.

"What?" I ask.

"Time is now, Arj," she says firmly.

I'm getting tense. Tense, I have plenty of tension already. "Listen, *group* is fine with me. I didn't mean to start any—"

"Yes, Marcus, *group* is fine," Eartha says, putting a

hand lightly on my shoulder, "but *coven* is probably more to the point."

It is as if all action in the room has ceased. Every head swivels, and everyone stares in our direction. I can feel my mouth hanging open.

Arj gets stern.

"A little *abrupt*, don't you think, Eartha? We do have a protocol."

They have a protocol. A coven and a protocol. They have words, definitions, semantics. I don't even have ground under my feet anymore.

"Maybe we should just have a cake and balloons and a banner that reads, Welcome to Blackwater, and By the Way, You're a Witch," she says.

Which is about all I need to hear.

"Wait," Eartha says as I make for the door.

"No," I say. "I feel like I'm intruding. I'll just see myself out, thanks."

"Please," Arj says, catching up and taking me, firmly, by the upper arm.

I stop, stare at his hand, then shake loose from him.

"All right, this is *enough*," I snap. "I don't particularly care what you freaks are up to down here. But you got no business pulling me into it."

"You're already into it," Arj says.

"Oh, really?" I say. "Well, watch me get right the hell back out of it." I stomp toward the door.

My hand is reaching for the knob, when from right over the top of me comes the green chair, missing my head by an inch before slamming into the door.

I turn around and stare. If it's down to a staring contest, then I lose, because several pairs of eyes are now peeling the skin right off me.

The temperature has fallen again. After a tense standoff, Eartha begins to approach me.

"Stay away," I say, holding both hands out in her direction.

Not only does she not advance on me, she retreats, as does everyone else. Like they are actually scared.

I've never scared anybody before, ever. At least, that I can remember.

I mentally catch a vision of myself. I have assumed a pose. Where I thought I was just holding up a stop sign, I have instead altered it slightly, so that all ten fingers at the end of my outstretched hands are pointing at her. I have never done this before, don't know why I'm doing it now. It appears to scare this collection of nut cases. I feel like an idiot.

"Shut up," I say, though nobody's said a thing. They follow my order, however, and shut further up.

I am out in the hallway and approaching the stairs at a trot when I hear Eartha calling me. I do not stop.

I have to get out of here. Not just here, the basement, the Key Club, the building. I have to get out of *here*, this school, this town. I feel this powerful pull on me, back to Port Caledonia, back to previous days, back to undo the foul whatevers back there in my past, so I can get out of this nightmare that seems to be punishing me.

I burst through the exit, to fresh air and real life and . . .

Eartha.

"How did you do that?" I demand. I am not even scared, exactly, though that makes no sense to me. I'm pissed off. "How did you *do* that, Eartha? You telling me you can *fly*, or walk through *walls* or something?"

She shakes her head. "Of course I can't."

"Good," I say, calming down only slightly. "You want to start talking sense *consistently* now, please?"

"Arj delivered me."

"Arj *delivered* you?" I bark, and am sort of ashamed of myself. Her eyes, Jules's eyes, are all warm and rounded at me. I don't talk to anybody like that. I have manners. Especially with her.

She is composed. "He moved me." She leans conspiratorially close. "*Moved* me, you know? You know about *moving*, don't you, Marcus?"

I nod, almost involuntarily. I am shaken, my stomach flipping. I am terrified that somebody knows. I am relieved that somebody knows. I want to touch her.

"The thing is, we need you, Marcus. And believe it or not, you need us as well."

"How do you know anything about me?"

She smiles, takes me by the hand, and leads me back inside.

"That's the kind of group we are. That's the kind of community you're in. We know. We watch. We watch out."

Petrified. Thrilled. Petrified. To say I have entered another world already would be to understate it badly.

When Eartha and I reenter the room, it is as if there is a flying circus being performed for our amusement. The card game I half witnessed earlier has been resumed. But the players are now spread out in a ten-foot-circumference circle, and the cards are changing hands continuously, rapidly, and all by themselves. The air among the players is alive, like a tank full of tropical fish, as bright, large playing cards swim every which way, players snagging them out of the air and then setting them free just as quickly.

The two Council members I had met, Baron and Winston, are pulling some form of telekinetic sumo wrestling. They stand three feet apart, and do nothing but stand, stare, glower. Nothing seems to be coming of it until gradually they begin leaning, leaning into each other as if into a hurricane wind, until it seems they have to fall into each other. They don't. They separate. Winston's feet, planted firmly, slip backward an inch. Two inches, ten inches. They are sweating, grimacing, and finally Baron lets out a barbaric sort of roar that sends Winston skittering across the floor like a downhill skier in reverse, until he is flat against the wall.

People are balancing books and pocket calculators and jockstraps in the air, all looking very serious and somewhat bored, until, out of the corner of my eye, I catch the sailing green blur and turn just in time to duck the chair as it whips once again over my head and cracks into the door. The green chair appears not to like me.

I turn to face Arj, but in the next instant the green chair has glided up behind me, buckling my legs. I am sitting, and the chair is moving, like a roller-coaster car, toward Arj. Just as it reaches him, it squeals to a halt. I sit, looking up at Arj, wondering where my life has gone. And where it will be going from here.

"You could have just asked him to come over," Eartha says dryly to him. "Drama queen."

"He needed to be shown."

Everyone has stopped juggling now and is gathering around me.

"Shown what? Your awesome power, right?" She is snappy, tough, and playful at the same time. She is, again, Jules. "Well, Marcus, there you have it, Arj's power. Show's over, 'cause there ain't no more. All he can do, more or less, is move stuff, same as everyone else in this room."

"Well," I say, still looking up at Arj, "I think it's pretty damn impressive."

"Thank you," Arj says, bowing to me and sneering at Eartha. "Everyone other than the Council of Youngers can now leave."

I get up out of my chair.

"Not you, Marcus," Arj says.

"Ah," I say, finding myself protesting very little with this guy, even though he does not seem in any way outwardly menacing. "So, are you, like, the head guy?"

They all laugh, until Arj turns on them, and everybody other than Eartha stops. He turns back to me.

"No, I'm flattered, but I'm not the head guy. But you're going to meet him. At the party on Friday night."

I cannot stand it. Of all the things I want to do (not many) and don't (plenty), a party is absolutely the most *not* thing on my list. I don't want to meet anybody else. I don't want to eat and drink, and I sure as hell don't want to be merry.

"A party?" I groan. "Listen, thanks, but . . . I don't have the stomach for it right now. I was hoping to just lay low this weekend, go for some walks with my dog, find someplace for fish and chips, play a little Brainwave . . . so, you know, if we could just conduct whatever *business* we have right here, I can just get out of your way and you can have your funky weird party on the weekend without me. Take pictures, though, 'cause I'll want to see. . . ."

It is a convincing effect, six heads shaking in perfect synchronization.

"No?" I ask.

"What do they speak, Caledonianian or something where you come from?" Baron barks. Jesus, this guy. If he gets this pissed off over me sitting in his chair, what would he do if I threw him across the room?

As if he is yanked by a cable around his waist, Baron suddenly jerks backward and crashes into a batch of empty chairs. He jumps to his feet. "Who did that?" he says, hands raised in that straight-out, palms-down quick-draw I used earlier.

Everyone in the Council is shrugging, shaking their heads, or giggling. "Come on," he says, louder. "Who's the witch bitch?"

Arj waves at him as if he's a football field away. When Baron looks at Arj, Arj draws his attention to me.

"Holy shit," I say.

"What?" Baron says.

"Better not piss the man off," Arj says happily.

Winston laughs. "Don't *make* Marcus kick your ass, Baron."

That does it. Baron is on his feet, marching toward me. He parts the group, which is happy to let him through. Thanks, guys.

He is very tense, Baron, and I am scared. "I don't really know how to do this stuff, I swear it."

Baron is thinking on his feet, which apparently is going to take a while. He turns to read the smiling faces behind him. Really, it's one of those *Murder on the Orient Express* deals where anyone could have gladly done the crime since the guy is such a piece of crap.

"Okay," Baron says finally. He stares at me a moment longer, apparently feeling he has to make more of a move before he can release me. "But if you sit in my green chair again I'm gonna kick your—"

The cable is jerked again, and Baron is folded tightly in half as he sails spine-first into the same unfortunate group of chairs.

Now there is not only laughter, but applause.

I feel my face turning red. "I didn't do it," I say, but nobody appears to believe me. "Did I?" I wonder out loud.

This is not my better self we are tapping here. I can't deny it, but there is a brand-new something surging up through me. Or if not new, something previously hidden. Like there is a power switch in me that is kicked on by just being in this room. I did that? I could do that? He deserved it. And I *gave* it to him.

I shouldn't enjoy that.

If only Baron weren't such an ass.

So then, if I could throw him twice, I could probably twist him by the—

"Don't get ahead of yourself," Eartha says, grinning and pointing at me.

"Christ," I say, feeling like I've been caught . . . well, *caught*. "You can see people's thoughts too. Great."

"No," she says. "You were either trying too hard or you were constipated."

Arj claps his hands loudly several times, and everyone takes this as a signal. We arrange ourselves in a circle, skipping the chairs altogether and squatting on the floor. Baron is slow to join.

"You coming?" Marthe asks.

I look over and see Baron still lying among the bowled-over chairs. "No," he says. "Start without me."

I for one am happy to start without him, if starting means finishing. I am out of my depth here and feeling it. I am alone in a crowd and more lost than I have ever been. Who am I? What am I? I want to be away from here. I am missing my mother and my dog.

"Let's start without him, for crying out loud," Winston says.

Better, I'd like to start without me. But this needs to happen. I need to know.

"Please, sit," Marthe says softly, half standing up and guiding me into a sitting position on the cold floor. Just the touch of Marthe's hands on my arm has a weird, soothing effect. She stares into me. "This must be really hard for you," she says.

"You must have a lot of questions, huh?" Winston says, offering me some kind of lozenge.

I recoil. "This some kind of witch thing? Going to

98

give me visions and make me writhe around the floor with a bloody dead chicken or something?"

Winston stares at his hand. "It's menthol eucalyptus. It's strong, but not that strong."

"You have us confused with voodoo," Marthe says as simply as if she were a librarian pointing me toward the ornithology section. "We are not"—she sniffs—"voodoo."

"What the hell are you, then?"

"We," Arj stresses. "*We*, Marcus. That's the first thing. We are a we. You are us and we are you and never the twain shall be cloven."

"There," I say, pointing at him. "There's a word. That's a bad one, right? *Cloven*. Hoofed? Evil, Satan, all that. This is one of those, right? Am I right? I don't want any part of that crap, folks, sorry. I mean it."

I am breathing heavily. Marthe is holding my hand, and Eartha is scowling at Arj.

"English," she snaps. "Plain old twenty-first-century English will get us through this, Arj."

"We are not devil-worshippers," Marthe says.

"But you say you're a coven," I point out to Eartha. "And you're telling me I'm a *witch*. For chrissake, a *witch*? That is so freaking corny."

Eartha shrugs. I look around the room. Nobody can do any better.

I shake loose from Marthe and bury my face in my hands. "You people are not helping me, okay? You're really, really not doing anything for me. Why am I here? Why am I even listening to you? I'll probably wake up tomorrow and see you all on the news eating babies or setting yourselves on fire or some such eerie crap."

There is a long gap in what is passing for conversation here. I don't even want to look up. I want to open my eyes and have them, and have it, and have every minute of the past week gone and my life and every life I have inadvertently banged into put back the way it was with a Band-Aid and a kiss on the head and may we all go our separate peaceful ways. I grip my face ever tighter like that guy in the *Scream* painting, and boy oh Jesus boy do I want to scream, until I am sure I am about to remove the entire covering of my flesh to reveal the blood and tissue and mucus of me spilling onto the floor.

I hear nothing, other than my own panting, moaning....

Then nothing.

Slowly, I remove my hands from my face. They are all gone. Except Marthe.

"We figured this might be too much, too fast," she says. For a Satanist, she has the aspect of an angel. She touches my arm again.

I jump up. "But of course you're sweet and lovely. What would I expect, a *serpent*?"

"We do wish you would calm down," she says.

"Yeah, well, I wish *you* would stop saying 'we.'"

She nods. "Point taken. You going home now?"

"Am I allowed?" I sound like the second rudest person in Blackwater.

"Yes," Marthe says, almost laughing. "May I walk with you for a while?"

I nod, and we make a quick exit.

Marthe walks me along the same winding, brush-heavy country roads and scrubbed, tidy-town streetlets that Eartha walked me along that morning. Every residential block of wood-framed, clapboard dollhouses is tree-lined, so that the hot-cold flashes of sun and shade are steady. "So why are you still here?" I ask. "Why aren't you gone with the rest of them?"

"I don't know," she says. "You tell me. You're the one who moved them all."

"Will you people stop saying stuff like that?" I say, waving my arms like a madman. "I didn't do anything with them. I don't know how to do something that big."

"Your modesty is charming," she says. "I think you should know, though, you're probably capable of a lot more than you think."

"What, the magic tricks? Big deal. Mumbo jumbo, and so what. There are magicians on TV who do more interesting stuff, like throwing playing cards through windshields and making the Statue of Liberty disappear. And *they* make mountains of money and sleep with supermodels for their troubles."

She goes all serene with me. *"An Obair,"* she says.

"Excuse me?"

"It's called An Obair, what we do, and it's not mumbo jumbo. It's Gaelic, and it means 'The Business.' It is our business, it is the stuff of our life. It is a magic unlike any other on earth."

I am flatfooted here. She is deeply serious, and I don't want her to be. She is unsettling, when I want her to be lovely, kind, and reassuring.

"Haven't you heard anything I've said?" I ask.

"About money and supermodels," she says flatly.

"Yes."

There is a pause. I fear she is not contemplating my words.

"An Obair is you, Marcus."

"The Business. Is me. I am The Business."

"You are."

"You know what," I say, shaking my head, staring at the lovely stream and trees and unclouded sky that now don't penetrate my quite clouded senses, "I hope I'm not. All this . . . whatever you people want to call it . . . it feels awful to me. If I am The Business, then I'm sorry, but we are *out* of business, okay? Even if I do have any kind of power, like you say—it doesn't seem to me to be such a terrific thing. Your creepy little group there making things fly, they don't seem to be getting themselves anyplace in a hurry. Why would I want to be like them? I don't have any interest in being Merlin or Harry Potter or Puff the Magic-freaking Dragon. I don't want to be any of all that. You know what I want to be? Alone."

She is shaking her head at me, but smiling, again, angelically.

"Right, but I can't, can I? Because we are *one*, our little freako society Key Club spooks. Well I don't want to be one. I want to be . . . well, *one*, but one by myself."

I know I am not helping myself. I am not solving anything. I am not ridding myself of their unwanted attention or these stupid unwanted powers, lame as they may be. And I am not *fixing* things. Things that I know need to be fixed.

I am fighting, but I am not clear on whom, what, or exactly why.

I need to get clear.

Angel Marthe stops, pulls me by the hand, and kisses me, fully, in the same way, in the same spot, that Eartha did this morning.

And I slow down. My thoughts, my flailing hands, my heart rate.

This does not feel bad. It should. Guilt and heartache, memory and loss, should be what I am flooded with now. I have none of it. I drift further out into the dream.

Am I ever awake now?

She releases me and regards me with the kindest almond-eyed understanding.

"What, then?" I ask slowly. "Am I to get the impression that witch girls are, like, all available all for me? And that's supposed to make it all better?"

She stares at me, waiting.

"Well, yes," I say, "it makes it better, but it doesn't make it *all* better."

Marthe either has incredible self-control—which the evidence suggests is not quite true—or she is unshakable. She is more patient than I deserve.

"We are not easy," she says. "We are *one*. And we are all we've got. If you think about it, you will come around to it."

I am shaking my head as we resume walking, because I am still quite some ways from coming around to it. But she certainly makes me want to try.

"I mean it, you know, that this Obair stuff doesn't

seem like such a wonderful thing. Whatever I have, I'd be happy to see it gone already. I'd do anything to get rid of it."

We walk.

She nods. "Everybody thinks differently about it. There are some people in our group, who hate it so much . . . you just want to put them out of their misery. There are others who just think it's a kick to be able to move stuff. And then there are, well, most of us, who think about the possibilities, think about the kingdom, the power and the glory, and they—"

"And you?"

"Me?"

"What, am I speaking Port Caledonian or something? Yeah, you. What is your vision?"

"Noted. Well. Well, well. All right, here it is. I think An Obair is art. I mean, *the* art. Because, you see, I write poetry, but not very good poetry, and I make sketches, which are better but not a lot better than the poetry, and I like to sing . . . but none of it . . . that is, all of it . . . It's all about limits, isn't it? Everything else, it's all about where it *stops*, about what you *can't* do. An Obair is art times a trillion. Art times infinity. Art times everything. The thought of having it, of having access to it, all of it, absolute unfiltered creative power . . . the art of essence, Marcus. It is our individual pieces of God. And you have a bigger piece than any of us.

"Have you ever wondered what you could do, if you could do anything at all?"

I am watching her as much as I am listening to her,

and small hotwires of Business crisscross my body from tip to tip. I don't believe it is possible to fake what Marthe is doing. I am, for the moment, willing to relax my rigid disbelief for her.

And if I do believe her?

What could you do, if you could do anything at all?

Do we really want the answer?

"An Obair," I say tentatively.

"An Obair," she says, "is the answer."

Where do you go from there in a conversation? Silent. We go silent for a while. We are approaching my house, and we veer off to sit on the bank of the stream. I throw rocks in as I talk, finally.

"How long have you known Eartha and Arj?"

"Years and years and years."

"And have they always looked like that?"

Marthe is about to throw her own rock. She stops and looks at me sideways. "Nobody always looks the same, Marcus, you know that. You getting freaky on me now?"

I probably am. Slowly it is coming over me that I am slipping between the cracks of two worlds—the one where people and boulders and cows do pretty much what you expect them to, and *this* world—and anything I say, anything I think I understand, will need to be checked at the door between those worlds.

But Marthe makes you feel like you can trust her. So you go ahead and be foolish.

"Do you know of any reason," I ask, "why one person should look to you like another person?" I throw bigger rocks, making bigger plunks in the water. "I mean, why, and how, would it be possible for one person, who you knew, so, who you really and intimately . . . so there is no mistaking that this is the face. . . ." I have to stop. In my mind, Jules's face is in my face. Her eyeballs are pressed to my eyeballs, her lips to my lips.

"You knew somebody. . . ." Marthe probes.

I nod.

"And you see her face."

I nod.

"Not just sort of."

I shake my head no, wildly, no. I throw a big rock, too hard, missing the stream completely and breaking a bottle on the opposite bank.

"Hmm," Marthe says thoughtfully.

She is holding back. I am as certain of it as I am of the water before me.

"Who is Eartha?" I say urgently. "Is she Eartha? Is she Jules? Will somebody finally tell me the truth about what is going on?"

I am holding her eyes. She cannot look away or throw a rock or drop off to sleep. If she is, as she seems, for real, Marthe is going to be the one to finally clue me in.

"Whoa," she says, lurching sideways, and glaring over my shoulder.

I turn to see a thick black snake squiggling through the air, then splashing down into the water.

"I moved it for you," she says. "It was—"

"I know," I say, sighing, "about to bite me. It does that."

"You need to watch that snake."

"I need to watch all snakes. Snakes suck."

"Yes, well, you need to watch that one more than the rest. That one has a temper."

I gesture wildly at the snake, at the squiggle crossing the midtempo current of the stream. "You *know* that snake, personally?"

Marthe does a nervous bit of double-take. "It's Eartha's snake." She looks across the water, searching. I look too, and there is no sign of it. "And it has big ears. Listen, Marcus, I should go now. We'll talk again."

I stand there, kind of frozen, watching Marthe as she scuttles up the bank, then stands, looking back toward the water.

Eartha's snake. A snake with ears. I should be surprised. I can't afford the luxury of surprise.

Up the bank in three steps, I catch up with Marthe. I stare hard at her, and the snake incident does not change a thing. "Please," I say, "Please?" I sound like a lost child, even to myself. "You were going to tell me . . . why I'm seeing Jules."

"I'm not sure, Marcus—"

"Please—"

"Right," Marthe says tentatively. "This girl . . . Jules? She was special, huh?"

I bite my lip. I grunt in the affirmative.

"Well, I'm not the most knowledgeable . . . that would be Arj—"

"I can't ask him!"

"Okay," she says gently. "Well, it sounds to me like you are haunting yourself."

"Haunting. Am I a ghost now too? What the hell?"

She is shaking her head. "No. *Terrorizing* yourself is probably more accurate. Listen, I can't tell you everything, but what I do know, and what you have to know, is that you are a very, very powerful individual, Marcus. You are capable of much more than you ever imagined. Much of what you see, you're controlling, whether you're fully aware of it or not."

I am a steady two beats behind her, trying to gather it all in, as every thought she utters becomes heavier for me to bear. I am staring at her beseechingly.

"Right," she says, reaching out and putting a hand on one of mine. "So if you are seeing things, seeing people, superimposing somebody over somebody else . . . there may be a good reason. You may be haunting yourself for something you might not even be sure of. The key question is, did you possibly do something very bad, something heinous to this person? Because if you had done something truly horrible—and I'm not saying you did—then sometimes what happens is that you begin to carry the person, trapped inside. . . ."

Marthe is talking, but I cannot hear her. I sink like a corkscrew into the soft wet earth of the riverbank, and grab the ground with both fists for balance.

But balance is a long way away.

6

We learn about the town by trying to get out of it.

The walks I've been taking—or been led on—have basically avoided the small town center of Blackwater. You can easily make it from my house to the school along the stream and through the residential and semirural bits of the area without ever knowing the center exists.

But if you want to get to the woods—and Chuck and I *want* to get to the woods—you have to cross the heart of Blackwater.

It's about the same as a lot of other tired, rustic, half-step-out-of-time town centers. It's shaped like a double cross, with the one main street and two lesser avenues crossing it. The shopfronts are as familiar as you can get; one bookstore, one hardware store, one barber shop complete with striped pole. There seem to be too many precious children's clothes shops. You could get your hair and your nails done in this town, you could visit three different realtors to buy a new house, or you could go to the bed-and-bath shop to spruce up the old one.

And every place you went to would look about the same, because the center of Blackwater appears to be one of those places where the look of all the shopfronts is dictated by some local ordinance. Except for the dilapidated old movie house that stands rotting like a big screw—an embarrassment to the Blockbuster video store next door—the whole place looks like it could be an old American theme park or a movie set with nothing going on behind it.

We meander through it, Chuck and I, following our noses to the woods. We can do that, could do it with our eyes closed. When it comes to woods and earth, air and water, my nose is every bit the instrument his is.

And what the nose finds, before it finds wood, is water. The scent of water, of the particles in the air, is never far away. It is like being at the ocean, except it is not salty water. I feel surrounded. There is the stream, burbling along out there somewhere, and a famous swimming hole, Blackwater Pond, out by the college, and there are little duck ponds and fountains, antique horse troughs and cement birdbaths dotted everywhere. They love their water in Blackwater.

Finally Chuck and I have found woods, a crest of evergreen humping up over the back end of town about a quarter mile beyond the THANK YOU FOR KEEPING

BLACKWATER TIDY—COME BACK SOON sign. We run the rest of the way.

We are, blissfully, breathing heavily once we reach them, taking forest essence deep into our lungs. I do not care if we ever emerge once we walk in. I really don't. Because we are at home the instant we step under the canopy, comfortable, cool, and familiar as it is.

"Maybe we'll build us a house in here, Chuck, whaddya say? Someplace where we can hide, where we can rule, where nobody can bother us . . . and we can't bother anybody else. Sounds good, you think?"

He thinks. But he shuts up about it. Atta boy, Chuck.

We walk steadily, as straight into the heart of the old growth as we can. We approach a solid-looking old pine tree with a nice shoulder about twenty feet up. I crouch down, and Chuck knows right what to do. It has been a while since he has been up a tree, and the excitement has him so charged he hurdles clear over me on the first try, then scrambles around for a second. He's on, and we are up.

I am back. Back in the air. Back to clarity, back to sense. Back, at least partly, to me.

"I don't think I can go to this party, Chuck. I don't think I believe a word these people say. An Obair? What the hell is that all about, The Business? They're giving *me* the business, is what it is. I have been sucked in so bad, Chuck . . . Chuck . . . stay still. . . .

"Chuck!"

I watch with horror as Chuck twists and bucks and plummets the twenty feet from the branch to the forest floor, crashing on his back.

He lets out a squeal and gets to his feet, hobbling in a circle, whimpering.

I scurry down the tree quick as a squirrel, but still not fast enough to catch him. He has taken off, limping all the way, back down the trail we just walked.

"Chuck," I call. "Chuck!" But despite his injury, he is losing me. I fall farther and farther back until, winded, I have to stop chasing him.

I am walking steadily, wheezing a bit, squinting to try to see him ahead, then checking the bushes immediately around me to see that he hasn't collapsed along the way.

"So, have you given it any more thought?" Eartha says from the bushes, scaring the absolute pants off me.

"Shit," I say, stumbling backward, away from her. I instantly regain my footing, if not quite my composure. "No, I haven't. I mean, yes . . . I mean, leave me alone, I have to get to my dog. Why are you people haunting me?"

I continue on the path toward home and listen, like a slasher-movie victim, to the determined padding of her feet behind me.

"Come on, Marcus," she says. "Wait up. Stop running."

"No. No, I want to be left alone. I need to be left alone. I need to know what happened in Port Cal, because I don't know what the hell is—" I stop dead, whirl around.

"Leave my dog alone," I shout. "We've been up a thousand trees together, and he never fell until *you* popped up. You witch."

This brings a faint smile to her lips. "Finally," she says, "you're getting it."

"I didn't mean that kind of witch. I meant the other kind. Bitch witch."

She is less amused. She actually looks hurt.

"Come on, Marcus, you don't mean that."

She takes a step closer. I take a step back. I am so lame, so vulnerable to her, I cannot be trusted. She looks wounded, speaks to me low in the Julesiest voice, and I start to melt like a snowman.

Stop, Marcus, think, stop, think, remember.

"Hey," I shout, startling her. "Is that your damn snake that keeps trying to bite me?"

"Don't take it personally," she says.

"Don't take it personally? It came all the way to Port Caledonia to bite me. That's pretty personal, isn't it?"

She takes a step closer. I take two steps back.

"Please, Marcus—"

"Please nothing. This is for starters. Tell me about the snake, or I'm gone. Tell me now."

She sighs. She sighs again. She shifts from foot to foot, looks behind her—everybody around here seems to be looking behind them. Mostly it's me.

"You had to come here, Marcus, and that is that. We needed you. And the snake—her name is Sonja, by the way—was there to make sure that you didn't make any last-minute mistakes before coming."

"For chrissake, what the hell could a snake . . . ?"

Here, right here, right now, something happens to me, from the inside out, from the top on down. It feels as if there is an actual fire burning on my inside, everywhere. Like lava is pouring through me, rushing from the hot center of my heart through my veins, through to every outer branch of my system. My eyes are bulging, as if the pressure inside my head has risen and will burst out through my skull, shooting my eyeballs across the forest.

"Juuuules!" I scream, and the woods shake with my rage. "Juuuuules!" I shake the ground again. I am nearly blind with this, and can see nothing as it is. It is as if I were flying, or, rather, as if I were standing still with the rest of the universe hurtling past me in strobes of brilliant white peripheral light.

Except for her.

I see the back of Eartha as she tries to beat a retreat away from me. Her long chocolate-brown hair is splayed out like turkey feathers as she attempts speed.

She achieves speed.

She flies, her feet leaving the ground as if some unseen giant bird of prey has swooped down, snagged her by the shoulders . . .

And thrown her, directly into the base of a giant, gnarly oak.

Next thing I know, I am standing over her. She is silent, writhing, shielding her face.

"Did your snake . . . ," I say, "have anything to do . . . ," I say, "with what happened to Jules?"

I could kill her. I could kill anyone, for the right reason, for the wrong answer, right now. I don't know who I am, but I could.

"She was just there," Eartha says in a trembling voice, "to get in the way."

"Why?"

"Because you weren't supposed to . . . do that."

"Why?"

"She was not your kind."

For the moment, for a change, for now, I am glad I have whatever powers I have.

"How . . . *dare* . . . you," I say, feeling the fire again, feeling my hands pulling into forged iron fists, feeling the trees shake again. . . .

Until Eartha flips herself over, lies on her back, arms and legs splayed out sacrificially, defenselessly, eyes closed. . . .

Jules's eyes closed. Jules's hair spread under her like a carpet.

I stand over her. I stand and I stare, and I stand and I stare. And the tremor slows, stops. My blood ceases boiling.

I know who I am. I feel who I am. I couldn't hurt anybody. I couldn't ever hurt this face.

But I am aware, as Eartha's eyes crack open, that my fists remain at my sides.

"Nobody means to hurt you, Marcus," she whispers, still terrified. "You will see that. We are only doing what has to be done—for you as well as for us. It's hard for you to see, but you will see. And besides, the snake didn't do anything. She was interrupted."

"I was interrupted."

"But not by us. There is a lot of power coming to you at this point."

I shake my head. I feel nothing like power in me

now. I feel weakness and confusion, and I am as vulnerable now as I was threatening just minutes ago.

"No," I say, "I won't see. Nothing good has happened to me since that night, my last night in Port Caledonia, and you and your people are all over it. I don't want anything to do with any of you from this moment on. I am going to find my Jules, and 'my kind' can just all screw themselves."

She is slowly, tentatively, shaking her head at me.

"Please don't do it," I beg, feeling like somehow I am pleading for both our lives. "Please don't make me mad, Eartha."

"I don't want to make you mad. I know, even more than you do, how bad that would be."

"Good. Let's just leave it at that, then."

I turn and take the first few steps in the direction of home.

"Not without us, Marcus. Without us you'll never f—"

I spin on her, one flat, extended hand held out in her direction. "I'm leaving now. I have to go take care of my dog. Leave us alone. Don't say anything, and don't follow me. I mean it, Eartha." I say it as if everything depends on it.

"Okay," she says, gently nodding. Nodding her lovely head. Jules's lovely head.

When I get back to the house, Eleanor is on the porch, seated in a big, sideways-slanted, white wicker armchair. Chuck is lying at her feet, looking like he has just finished a game of rugby as she pats him down, smoothing and soothing him.

"He's awfully spooked," she says as I mount the steps.

Chuck raises his head and looks at me, his eyebrows raised emphatically.

"Is he?" I say, sliding right up beside him, waiting my turn.

The three of us stay there silently, solidly, for a very long time.

On Friday morning I make my decision.

"Mr. Sedaris?"

"Yes, Marcus, please come in."

Mr. Sedaris, my guidance counselor, has a very kind, reassuring face and manner. He is about five feet seven inches tall, with frizzy black hair and one eyebrow. He wears a blue-and-green plaid sweater that reaches to his Adam's apple, so you can't quite tell if he is wearing a tie, but I am guessing he is not. This immediately sets him apart from the sedate Blackwater faculty.

"Thanks for stopping by, Marcus. I was hoping you would. I normally like to have a more extended meeting with new transfers, but heck, you saw what it was like on registration day—nutsy, wasn't it? Have a butterscotch hard candy."

"Thanks," I say, though it is barely a hard candy. I must be the first one to accept the butterscotch offer in a while. As I take it, it dents under the hardly viselike pinch of my fingertips. And when I try to peel back its transparent yellow wrapper, it clings to the paper as if it is embarrassed to be naked.

"And I have a hunch you need a fair bit of guidance around here. No?"

"Yes," I say.

"I know my kids. Now, how are you settling in?"

"Well, to be honest—"

"No," he says, covering his ears and jumping out of his seat. "No, don't do *that*."

I stand to leave. I am fairly easily derailed at this point.

"I'm joking," he says, waving me down. "You're a very serious fellow, Marcus. What are you, like, a poet or something?"

"No. Actually, Mr. Sedaris, I only wanted to talk to you about my schedule."

"Oh. Well, okay. I was kind of expecting something a little more challenging, but . . . okay, you want to change something. What do you want to change?"

"All of it."

"All of it. Hmm, all of it. All of it? That's a very unusual request, Marcus. Why would you want to change your entire schedule? I see, for instance, you're in Spanish. Spanish is the second language of the United States, and getting bigger all the time. You'll do well with Spanish. Can't go wrong there. And study hall. Who the heck would want to dump study—"

"I'm just feeling a little crowded. In my current schedule. Like I can't get any space."

"You know, all the class sizes are the same, pretty much. Except Latin. You'd have a lot of elbow room in Latin. You want Latin?"

This is not going very well at all. In my state of distress, I think I have once again miscalculated the workings of things. I actually somehow thought I was going to skip into Mr. Sedaris's office, tell him to change everything on my schedule only one week into the year, and he was going to fix me up and send me on my way with nary an inquiry into my motives. Not only is that not happening, but he is, deliberately or otherwise, making it hard for me to get through the conversation.

"It's not about class size. Can I speak frankly, Mr. Sedaris?"

"No," he says again, covering his ears again. "Don't do *that*."

With as much respect as possible, I say, "Could you stop that, please?"

"Sorry," he says. "I just like to break the tension. A lot of tension comes into my office, as you might imagine. You brought a load of it in yourself, did you not?"

"I did."

"Okay, so, you being bullied?" he asks sternly.

"No."

"Harassed by faculty?"

"No."

With each wrong answer, Mr. Sedaris leans harder over his desk, in my direction, as if he will read the right answer in the ever deepening lines of my troubled teen face.

And the further he leans toward me, the further back I tip my chair in the opposite direction.

"Overwhelmed by the coursework?"

"No. If I may just—"

"No, no, don't tell me. I can do this."

I sigh, leaning back far enough that my toes are just about keeping contact with the floor.

He gets a eureka face.

"Got it. It's the strain and confusion of discovering you are a witch."

I make a huge clatter as I fall, first backward, then as I catch the edge of his desk with my toes, forward. I land with my palms flat on Mr. Sedaris's desk, and my face in his face.

"Did I get it?" he asks, all excited, as if he honestly isn't sure.

I gulp. "Pretty close, yeah."

"Told you I knew my students. Now, why exactly do you want to escape?"

This is the latest in a lengthening line of don't-know-which-way-to-go forks in my road. Who is a friend, and who is a foe? Is anyone really either one, or should I just take my chances and beat it the hell out of here? How much of what has happened to me—if any of this has actually happened to me—is my own fault?

"You can talk to me, Marcus."

"How do I know that? If you already know . . . about me, then you're obviously one of them, right?"

"Us. One of us, you mean. That's the point. That's why you do not have to be afraid, ultimately. Because we are us. You are inside now, not outside. And you have never been inside before, have you, Marcus?"

"I am not afraid," I say. I am scared out of my mind now. "I am cautious, that's all."

"Cautious is good," he says, leaning back to appear less threatening. "Under the circumstances, cautious is wise.

You go on being cautious. But I want you to know that I am your guidance counselor for school, and for the *other*, as well."

"Great," I say, a wave of frustrated aggression coming over me. I lean over his desk. "Counsel me then. What's going on?"

"Go to the party, Marcus."

"What, am I supposed to bring the snacks or something? Why does everybody keep telling me to go to this freaking party?"

"Just go to the party, okay? You'll know a lot more when you go to the party. You'll know a lot more, and then I'll be able to counsel you the way I should."

I swear, this is the last person I am going to talk to. I swear. I make a note to myself not to talk to people. *Don't talk to people, Marcus. Ignore everybody. By playing, you are letting them do this to you.*

Don't play anymore.

"What about my schedule?" I say as I am about to go out the office door.

"They are merely looking out for you," he says.

"What about my *schedule*?" I demand, as if I had the slightest bit of power or control over anything.

He shrugs. "Whither thou goest, they will follow. Better to be shadowed in Spanish and study hall than—"

I slam his door as he speaks.

I have lost all my manners on top of everything else.

"Eleanor?" I call as I enter the house. "Eleanor? Chuck?"

The place is wide open and dead quiet. The sound of

the water running past the rear of the house is clear and almost soothing in the absence of anything else. Except that nothing is quite soothing anymore. I take a walk around the first floor, the living room, the kitchen, the hallway. There is nothing going on, and no sign that anybody has been around for a while. Not even Chuck, which doesn't make a lot of sense, since Chuck's social life is marginally more stagnant than mine.

Than mine used to be, that is. How I long for my stagnant social life.

I go to the foot of the stairs and call once more. "Eleanor. Chuck."

Nothing. She must have been really going stir crazy if she took Chuck for a walk. Or maybe they are just bonding.

At any rate, it is a sensation that takes a little getting used to. As far as I can recall, I have never been in the house, either house, without at least one of them being there with me. I don't like it.

I go out to the porch and watch the water flow by, the nearest thing to a living breathing companion I have at the moment. My sudden loneliness is, I realize, ironic, with all the *being alone* I'm always wanting. But what I want is to be alone, but with my familiar beings close to hand.

I need my Eleanor, as I figure she needs me. Just on the other side of the wall. And I need my Chuck.

I gingerly put my feet up on what's left of the rail and try to make like a regular, slow and easy country gentleman. The stream, the pitiful breeze, the occasional bird. Thus, the world goes by. Nothing moves that isn't supposed to move. Nobody says anything that contradicts the physical world I knew the first sixteen years of my life.

I need to spend more time here. On this porch.

I am not going to any parties. Nothing more can happen to me if I just stay put.

Bang. It comes from upstairs. I get to my feet.

Bang, it happens again, and again, as if somebody is pounding the walls with a two-by-four.

I slowly walk into the house. I walk to the bottom of the stairs and wait there, the way you wait when things go bump in the night and you want to give the silence every chance to explain. *I was asleep it was a cat the wind blew off a shingle it was a dream a truck hit a pothole or a cat my mother nodded off into her computer car backfired on the next block.*

The mercy of silence continues another ten seconds.

Bang.

I have to go up. I can see my hands shaking in spite of the mighty fists I am making.

"Chuck?" I call. "Eleanor?"

Nobody responds.

I reach the top of the stairs, and my eyes shoot straight down the hall to the open door that leads to the attic stairs and the dim light at the summit. This is not unusual. I come home every day to find that door open. I've still never gone up there. I merely close it. Then, when I come up to bed later in the night, I close it again. Not unusual.

Bang. This is unusual. The door closes itself. Then opens slowly and *bang*, closes itself.

The door is mad at me now.

"I don't give a rat's ass who you are or what tricks you can do. I'm not coming up there."

It slams again and again and again.

I stand there, like a child who cannot cope with the world, hands covering my ears, eyes shut tight to the world, whatever world. "Shut up!" I shout.

No deal. The door slamming gets louder and more frequent, until it becomes one long loud unbroken crash, like a car accident played on a loop, and there is no escaping it, no stopping or muting or eluding it and so what I have to do is just . . .

Absorb it. I drop my hands to my sides, unsquint my eyes, and let it come.

"Come, bastard," I say, and the bastard comes, I can feel it.

"Come, evil bastard," I say, feeling something, something like strength, rising inside of me, and the bastard comes, rising, approaching, filling me. I am being entered from without by something, something foreign, something that wants to overwhelm me, but I cannot fold. Not here, not here, not in my house after which I will have nowhere left. . . .

I wait for more and realize this is it. I am available and prepared for more, but this is what comes, this is the extent of what can happen to me.

Because I'm not buckling. I'm not fleeing or cracking.

"Come. Come on, evil, impotent bastard," I finally shout.

And the bastard quits.

There is no more slamming. And there is no next move. I can even hear the water again.

I walk to the door, stand in the doorway, and look up. I have achieved something, passed a test, called a bluff. Something bizarre may be happening around me after all, but it is not a great and powerful something. That's what I say. I am surrounded by tricksters, jugglers and clowns, noisemakers and shadow puppeteers.

I won't be afraid, and that will be the end of it.

I reach in, pull the string and kill the light. . . .

And illuminate the eyes . . . of something, I don't know. . . . I slam the door myself this time and lean against it, then . . . no, no, get away from the door. Victims always lean against the door. . . .

My chest is heaving as I stumble into my room. I close my door, grab for my chair. The machine is now on, and I am focusing, staring, listening so hard to the game starting up that I wouldn't notice if there were a werewolf chewing on my ear. As if I'm in a tunnel, private and secret and deep and mine alone, I hurtle down through the protective depths of my game, away from all that is above and behind me. I find myself levels and levels deep into Brainwave, kicking ass left and right. I am great, I am sublime. I am untouchable. More than anything untouchable. The muscles at the base of my thumbs are tight and throbbing from work.

I pause the game. I pause myself. Then I look down.

Chuck is at my feet.

"Hi, Chuck," I say, in a voice so disconnected and filtered through mania that the words should be "Take me to your leader."

Chuck's big droopy eyes are dripping with pity for me. I'll take it.

I get up, step over Chuck, and walk the length of the hall. No Eleanor, but her computer is humming.

I am not walking on any stairs, ever again in my whole life, without calling out first.

"Eleanor?"

"Marcus Aurelius."

I have rarely been so pleased to hear my stupid name.

When I reach the kitchen, she is happily working away, stir-frying a bunch of vegetables and soft noodles, tossing shrimps and scallops and big chunks of ginger root around in between sips out of a red wineglass that is really more like a fishbowl with a stem on it.

"Darlin'," she drawls. Happiness conjures up her North Carolina roots. Happiness and wine combined.

"Hey," I say, taking in the great smells, the sizzle, and the crackly old R&B out of the countertop radio.

"I thought I would make us a special ol' dinner tonight, celebrate our surviving the first week, reaching Friday night and the weekend in one piece."

She pours me a normal-sized glass of wine, hands it over.

"Also, I've got a little department get-together, and you've got that party, so it'll be good for us to have a healthy meal behind us, to launch our first real night on the Blackwater social scene."

"I have a what?"

"'Cause it would be a shame if after all this you wound up going the same recluse route you were taking in Port Caledonia. This is going to be the best thing for us ever, I can just—"

"I'm not going to any party, Eleanor," I snap, dumping myself into a kitchen chair.

She places a steaming, peppery plate in front of me, a riot of colors with red and orange and yellow peppers, snow peas, soy-soaked water chestnuts.

"What do you mean you're not going? You're the one who just told me about this thing not a half hour ago."

"The hell I am," I say, spearing a shrimp with my fork. What? Now I'm having conversations that I'm not even present for?

"Please, Marcus, don't be like this. Get out there and mix. Just give it an honest try."

Eleanor uses chopsticks. It is hard to tell quite what she's using them for, since very little food makes it to her mouth.

"They're all freaks here, Eleanor. I don't need it."

"Well, you need something. You can't just—"

"I have you," I say sweetly, trying to take a few years off my face with an extrawide smile.

"Yes, well, you will have me anyway. You need peers."

"I have Chuck."

Eleanor appears to be taking this a great deal more seriously than I would have expected. My social seclusion has never been big news or a big problem. She picks at her food with just one chopstick. She picks more successfully at her wine.

"You," she says sternly, "would do well to fit in. Now, I'm no fan of conformity . . . and I think it's great to go your own way like you do. It's just that it might be nice to see that you have the option. That you can be a member . . . of one society or another if you want to. There's more to life than the woods, Marcus." It is important to her. Having said her bit, she now seems to have trouble even looking at me. I can't bear to watch her struggle any longer. I get up and go over to the silverware drawer. I sit back down, hand her a fork.

"I'll try," I say.

She smiles.

"But I'm not going to start with this party. I'm just not into it."

She nods. We both sip wine.

"I feel bad," she says apologetically. "And now, here . . . you don't even have Jules. . . ."

She doesn't mean to hurt me, just as I don't mean to hurt her. But it's two people talking. It just seems inevitable.

I would love right now to burst out of the chair, stand proudly and announce, "Ah, but I do—I found her and she loves me and we are staying together for ever and ever." For both our sakes—all three of our sakes—I would love to be able to say it.

But I can't. It isn't true.

The phone rings. I get up and retrieve it from its mount on the wall. I listen.

"Yes, this is me."

I am looking at my mother as I talk. She beams, that I am receiving a phone call. That is how bad it is.

"Jule—" I catch myself. I quickly correct myself. "Sorry, Eartha." It comes out hard. The effect, on the phone, is doubly powerful—that voice is Jules's voice.

"Eartha," Eleanor mouths. She toasts me with her glass, as if this is some mighty achievement on my part.

"Just calling to make sure you are coming to the party," Eartha says.

"No. Actually, I wasn't feeling up to it. Thanks anyway. Maybe another time."

"Please, Marcus, you have to stop this now. You know that this is important. You know everyone is expecting you and that you are the whole point."

I am the whole point. Inwardly, I moan.

"I appreciate that, I really do, Eartha. But I really don't think I'm up for all this. Not tonight."

There is a long deathly silence on the phone. I turn my back to Eleanor's disappointment and stretch the long, white, curly cord as far down the hall as it will go.

"Leave me alone," I whisper.

"Come to the party," she pleads.

"Leave me alone," I repeat.

"Listen," she says, "Things are going to be really bad, if you don't—"

I gasp. I'm not frightened. Not more than I am every day now anyway. I am stunned.

"What's this, a threat now? You are threatening me?"

"I am doing no such thing. I am just giving you an

idea . . . of the way things can be, will be, for the likes of us."

"The likes of us." I snort. "I am not the likes of you."

"Like it or not," she says.

There is nowhere else to go, it seems. After we wait each other out for a few more seconds, I break the silence.

"Listen," I say. "I have a really nice dinner getting cold. I'll see you at school on Monday, and you can tell me all about it."

"Your Familiar would like you to come," she says quickly.

"What?"

"Your dog, Chuck. He's your Familiar. We all have them. It's kind of like a good-luck charm . . . except one that knows every corner of your soul too. You know."

"Well, no, I don't know," I say, and I feel like I am half lying here, "but . . . right. And how do you know my dog wants me to go to this party?"

"Well, Marcus, because he's here."

I am about to blow. I grind my teeth, grip the phone as if I can choke the life out of it. I am about to launch, to tear into Eartha and the whole lot of them . . . when suddenly I am awash, in the feeling that I can say nothing, nothing that will do anything.

I collapse against the wall with my shoulder pressed against it, and sigh a growly sigh at her.

"You know, you people are really beginning to piss me off."

"I know," Eartha says gently. "And believe me, Marcus, the last thing we want is for you to be angry. It's just that it's important for us to get you here."

"Good-bye," I say, after Eartha has given me directions to the party. I hang up before she can jerk another knot in my brain.

I am sitting quietly with Eleanor. I must have been on the phone for a while, because my dish is newly heated.

"Thanks," I say.

She smiles kindly, half-refills my glass, then her own. She catches a drip with her fingertip and licks it off.

I take a mouthful of noodles and bite into a hunk of ginger, which I usually love. But not now. I cannot eat any more.

I put down my fork, stand, and wipe my mouth with my napkin.

"What?" Eleanor asks, getting up as well. "What's the matter?"

"Nothing," I say, the latest in a growing series of big, flabby, fat lies. "I have to get going to that party."

She perks up, raises her glass. "That's the spirit, Marcus Aurelius."

I drain my glass.

"Yeah," I say.

CHAPTER

7

The party, symmetrically enough, is at Arj's house. His house is one essentially straight mile and a half from mine, on the same piece of waterway. Only by the time it reaches Arj's place, the stream has grown up—broadened, deepened, acquired a seriousness you wouldn't guess at from my sleepy, dreamy back veranda.

I follow the water the whole way. It is a lovely route, but it doesn't seem to be the most practical, since my shoes are half waterlogged by the time I arrive.

As I walk up the long graceful slope from the riverbank to Arj's residence, I notice a definite difference between this party and the last one I attended. It is quiet. So quiet I am not sure I have found the right place, until I determine that if I have missed it, I have missed it profoundly. I cannot even see where the next house might be, in any direction, and I decide right here that if this is not it, I am passing on this party once and for all and I am sorry, my lifelong friend Chuck, but you are going to have to go on your own wits to get out of this because mine are AWOL.

But as I go to ring the doorbell and the door swings open for me all on its own, I figure I probably have the right place.

The entrance hallway, long like a tunnel cut into a mountain, is lit by nothing other than about five hundred candles sprouting up from growing wax mounds along the floor. The hallway is bigger than the entire house appears to be from the outside. The floor is honey-colored marble, and the carved white-plaster ceiling floats twenty feet above. To my left is a stairway leading, eventually, into blackness, with an ornate iron bannister that looks like an endless, busy, roiling Celtic knot. To my right is a black onyx shelf about eight inches deep and six feet long sticking out from the wall. It is neatly lined with tall, frosted glasses, vine etched and with stems of pewter. All the glasses are full of poppy champagne bubbles, and I do not think twice about taking one and walking down the hallway.

"Hello?" I call, to any and all of the dozens of closed doors I see.

"You should really take those off," Eartha says behind me, tapping me on the shoulder.

I turn around, and she is standing there in a gold and black and purple and green tunic, floor length, embroidered and beaded so that it looks like something between a priest's Lenten vestments and a Mardi Gras float. Her thick hair is completely tamed, every single strand pulled into one of a hundred fine braids, the braids then turned into a pattern like a crop circle. She is smoking an ivory pipe about a foot long.

She is pointing at my shoes.

"It would hardly be a party for you if you went squishing around in wet shoes all evening."

I cannot reconcile the vision of her with the absurdity of discussing wet shoes.

"My god," I say. I am gawking.

"Yeah? You like it?"

"My god," I say. I am addressing, first, her appearance, which is so stunning I am getting a headache. But I am more broadly addressing . . . everything. I take a sip of my champagne, attempt to pull myself together.

"My dog," I say, one step closer to functioning.

"Oh, he's great. Having a ball. He's telling jokes and stories, and somebody brought a sheep, and they're really hitting it off. . . . Why don't you take those shoes off?" She points to her own foot, extended to show off her naked dog with silver rings on all five toes.

"Well, I won't be staying long, so the shoes won't really be a prob—"

"You want a hit?" she asks, extending the pipe.

Whatever is in the bowl smells like toffee and sandalwood and peat and a half dozen of the most caressing scents I have experienced, along with many more I have not.

"No, thank you," I say.

"Then would you mind holding it for a second?" she says.

134

I take the pipe reluctantly, and as I do the smoke begins funneling toward me, the way it does when you are the only one in a restaurant not smoking. It has an uncommon, appetizing smell that makes me want to go for it, though I have never deliberately inhaled any smoke in my life. I am furtively inhaling it anyway, and watching the greenish smoke trail the way a cobra watches a snake charmer, when I realize what Eartha is doing.

She is down on her knees, and has unlaced both of my shoes. She has, without my even noticing, removed one shoe and one sock, and as I look down at her, she looks up at me. I lift the second foot so she can finish.

"There," she says, rising, taking back the pipe, and standing toe-to-bare-toe with me. "Isn't that nicer? You wouldn't want to be the only one in the place with shoes on anyway, would you?"

I look all around us and listen hard.

"We appear to be the only ones in the place, shoes or no," I say.

Eartha giggles. She steps a bit closer, then stands with both feet on mine, and kisses me lusciously.

"There are spirits all around us," she says then, gesturing theatrically. She laughs again, looking at my feet.

I look down and see one silver ring, knotted much like the railing, on the second toe of each foot.

"Thanks," I say.

Eartha puts her pipe down on the onyx shelf and leaves it there like just one more open-house party favor waiting for the next arrival. Then she takes up two more flutes of champagne.

I finish off my glass, take the new one, then follow as she leads me by the hand.

"You ready?" she asks as we approach a door.

"I haven't the slightest idea whether or not I am ready."

She turns, for the moment darkly serious. "Before . . . before anything, know this—nobody here wants to hurt you or do you any kind of harm whatsoever. You have absolutely nothing to be afraid of here. You are ours, you are us, and you are special. You understand that?"

I understand nothing.

"It seems to me that if somebody is going to *really* hurt you, the first thing they do is to say they're not going to hurt you."

She is serene. "Is that the way you feel now, Marcus? Is that what you feel is going to happen now?"

I am looking into her eyes, into Jules's eyes, even if she is not Jules. I am looking into them so deeply, more deeply than is probably wise, so deeply I am in danger of toppling in, disappearing headlong into the unreality there. I know this is not wise. I am powerless.

"I want Jules," I say.

"If you want me to be Jules, I am Jules."

"I don't want you lying, is what I want. I want you honest. I want you to stop feeding me nonsense."

"No lies, no nonsense. What you want here is what will be."

The smoke still hangs in the air. As does the silence.

"I want my dog," I say.

"So be it," she says. "Pick a door."

I look up and down this impossible hallway. The doors are all the same, nine feet tall, narrow, and grainy matte black, like they are constructed of stone. It is all neat, orderly, utterly unpromising, and scary.

"I pick," I say dubiously. "Any one."

"Any one," she says.

"That one," I say, pointing to the one that actually faces us, at the far end of the hallway.

"No. Sorry. Pick another."

"Jesus," I say. I then pick the one closest to it, at the end of the hall, on the right.

"Off we go," she says, taking my hand in her over-warm, creamy soft one.

When we get to the door and still I hear nothing, sense nothing like a party going on beyond any door, I turn to Eartha. She is no help. Grinning, squeezing my hand, gorgeous. But no help.

I throw the heavy door open wide, to reveal nothing.

Nothing, that is, except what I was after. My dog, sitting at the center of a huge, empty, black-walled room. Licking himself.

I turn again to Eartha.

"How did you know I would pick the right door?"

"Because any door you pick is the right door."

"Cut the crap and give me real answers, will you?"

"That is the real answer. It is as I told you. There is a lot more power in you than you know."

I pull my hand away from hers. "And I don't *wanna* know. I'm outta here. Come on, Chuck."

Very casually, Chuck finishes grooming, and saunters

out of the room as if he is stoned. His eyes are red and droopy, he's grinning, and he's in no hurry whatsoever.

I slam the door shut, hand my empty glass to Eartha, and head for the front door.

She is not trying to get me to change my mind, which is surprising, and a relief. And maybe a bit of a disappointment.

But as always with these people, there is a reason. As I am almost out, I hear it. It comes so much out of nowhere that I stop short in front of the front door. Where before the house was a great silent spooky nothing, another joke waiting to spring on me, this door holds something different, even though I know it's the door I came in through. It sounds like a party.

Another door slams behind me. I turn, and she is gone.

The door immediately in front of me has a peephole in it, the way a normal house would have on an outside door.

I take a peek.

There is fat and ornate overstuffed furniture scattered about the huge ballroom. The colors are rich—burgundy drapes, gold-leaf wallpaper, cobalt-and-black oriental carpets that look about four inches thick. There are forty or so kids my age swishing around to some weirdly compelling music, something baroque played on electronic instruments. The scene looks to me like what I'd imagine a state dinner at the White House would look like if they had one for only under-twenty-ones.

Chuck is scratching at the party door.

"You really think we should?" I say.

He continues scratching.

"Stop that," I say, then try the fat brass knob. "When did you get to be such a party dog?"

Before I am even fully through the door, I am locked in a mad embrace. I am squeezed, then I am kissed, by Marthe.

"I am so glad," she says. Then she lets go and turns to reveal the room.

Which is a different room from the one I saw through the peephole.

It is filled with smoke. It is a quarter of the size I thought it was. There are four mismatched sofas that look like they were rejected from everybody's basement. The walls are not gold leaf but are, instead, blackboards, with writings scrawled all over, maps and caricatures and mathematical formulae and a recipe for Arj's Wondrous Oatmeal Wormwood (WOW) Cookies.

Nobody's dancing. People mostly flop on the sofas, on the floor, on each other. The entire place is one large makeout scene in various forms of grapple.

"Come on in, mingle, feel your way around," Marthe says. "I'll go get you a drink and a cookie."

"Just a drink," I say quickly. "I had wormwood for supper."

She is gone, and I do mill around. I walk the room like a ghost, a ghost and his dog, as nobody seems to appreciate that we are here. I can vaguely figure out who some of these people are, but most are unfamiliar to me. I figure they are all Key Club members, but none, besides Marthe, are from the Council of Youngers.

"Here you go," Marthe says, handing me a cup of

something that may be blue. The lighting in the room is sort of four giant lava-lamp columns burbling in the corners, so shadows and definition come and go.

"What is this?" I ask.

"Arj's Blue Brew," she says, motioning me to try it.

"I don't think so," I say.

"Don't be like that," she urges. "We love you here. We wouldn't let anything happen to you."

I gesture around the room, toward all the writhing bodies. "Love is kind of devalued around here, if I may say so."

Marthe's ever-present smile falls away. She nods grimly. "You don't approve of us, do you?"

This, I think, is a bit much. Not only am I not used to large groups of people seeking my approval, I have trouble even comprehending how my opinion could matter to them at all.

"*Approve* of you? I don't even know what the hell you are."

"Yes you do."

"No," I say, defiant. "I do not."

She is looking at the drink, and pouting.

I take a sip.

I feel, instantly, the blood rushing to my head, my eyes getting blinkered.

"Damn," I say, handing the glass back to her. "Sorry. No offense, but your drink is nasty."

"Oh, this isn't going very well at all, is it?"

"Don't worry about it," I say. "I wasn't planning to stay long anyway."

"Your dog seems to have gone off again. Maybe you better go find him."

"Crap," I say, looking back at the open door.

I can't say I am sorry to leave that room, but I have no interest in exploring Arj's funhouse.

"Chuck," I call from the hallway, and though he refuses to answer, I catch sight of the end of his tail as he heads up to the second floor.

"Damnit, Chuck, no," I say, as I follow reluctantly.

I get to the top, and find no Chuck. I find no doors. I find no light. It is as black as blackness gets, and I find myself frozen in place with fear. I am suddenly very cold, though it is a hot, sticky night.

"Chuck?" I call softly.

"What?" is the reply.

"Who is that?" I ask. "Who's there?"

"I am," the voice says. It's a guy's voice, and I have heard it before, but I cannot place it.

"All right, that's very funny, but I just want my dog. Can I have my dog, please?"

With a pop, lights come on, so bright it is like I am on television, and I have to shield my eyes and wait for the spots to go away. When my vision clears, Baron is standing in front of me. We are in a glistening porcelain room, a sort of oversized bathroom but without the fixtures. The bright harshness of the place highlights the hard angry angles of Baron's gaunt face, his prominent pointed jaw, his severe, slicked-forward hair. We stand about eight feet apart, like gunslingers.

"Didn't think you were going to show," he says.

"Neither did I," I say.

"Glad you did, though."

"Really?" I say. "That doesn't appear to be true."

"Well then, you're mistaken. I'm more anxious than anyone to see you. Because I can't wait to prove you're not what you say you are."

I spit out a bitter laugh. "What I *say* I am? What the hell do *I* say I am? I never claimed to be anything, and you know what, if you freaks will just leave me and my dog alone, I'll just disappear all over again, right on out of your little Dungeons and Dragons game."

"I wish it were that easy. But nobody else is going to let that happen. You're too *special*."

I have a building pounding feeling in my chest, a feeling that if I do not get out of here as soon as possible, I am going to regret it.

"Where is my dog, Baron?"

"He's that way, bro," Baron says with a leer. He is pointing behind him, where there is, of course, a door.

"Oh, what," I say, "tough guy, big man, I have to go through you to get there, right? What are you trying to prove?"

"I got nothing to prove. You're the one. *The One*, I should say."

"One what?"

"It. The Man. The Chosen."

I don't care what he is saying, what he is expecting, what he is challenging me to do. I am walking around him and getting my dog.

"You're an ass, Baron," I say, attempting to brush past him.

He steps into my path. "I ain't kidding you. You're supposed to be our Messiah, man!"

He has me frozen, his face right in mine.

"You are pathetic," I say. "The whole bunch of you."

I make one more move toward the door, but he won't let me get to it. He has me by the shirt and is hissing vile ammonia breath in my face.

"Great, you're a big man," I say. "What do you expect me to do?"

"Something!" he yells. He sounds almost as if my failure disappoints him. "*Look* at you. Arj thinks we can't do better than *this*? Do something, Messiah. Something. Anything."

I decide I cannot disappoint him.

I spit at him. I may not be The Chosen whatever, but I can hock a chunky spit with the best of them. I catch him right in the mouth.

I am laughing out loud when he punches me with a straight left hook that drops me to the floor.

I reach up to my mouth and feel the split in my lip. But there is no blood.

"So what're you gonna do?" he asks, standing, waiting. "Huh? Go on, throw me out the window."

"There is no window."

He is shouting now. "So make a window and throw my ass out of it! Do something to show me that you are The One, and I swear I'll be the first bastard down on his knees kissing your feet. I swear it."

As enticing as that offer is, I cannot do it. Because I am not it. Just like he says.

What I can do is get to my feet, get to that door, and get my dog. I need, *need* my friend Chuck.

I walk. Baron warns me not to, and still I walk. He bumps me hard with his chest. I back up, squint my eyes, push forward, bang into him again.

I don't know what to do. I am in this catacomb of blackness and perversion, I am lost and I am alone in a way I never in my wildest imaginings ever dreamed of, and I am very scared and my friend, my dog, my true spirit companion is on the other side of that door and I cannot get there to save my life.

I squeeze my eyes closed and wait for the worst, hope, perhaps, for the worst, for Baron to knock me into some province of oblivion where at least nobody is going to ask me what I'm going to do next.

Instead of the fist through me, I feel arms around me.

"I can't do too much of this," Mr. Sedaris says. "The physical contact thing. This can get a counselor into some hot water." He is patting my back firmly.

I push away from him, step back. I am in his office.

"Maybe you should sit," he says.

I fairly crash into the seat. Mr. Sedaris calmly takes the seat next to me.

"What is happening to me, Mr. Sedaris? Am I raving? Am I gone completely?"

"No, I think you're fine, and you will remain fine. Unless you drank the blue stuff. You didn't drink any blue stuff, did you?"

"Mr. Sedaris," I snap.

"Listen, Marcus, you just need to calm down, first of all. You're so freaked you're not listening, watching, feeling what is going on around you. Yes, there is something serious going on. But you can handle it."

"I don't *want* to handle it."

"You, above all, can handle it."

"Stop *saying* that. I want you all to stop saying that. Don't make me out to be something I'm—"

"Marcus," he says, much more sternly than usual, and seizing my face in his hands. "Your first job is to believe it. Get out of your own way and believe it."

I blink, exactly once.

And Arj is the person in front of me, holding my face in his hands. He kisses me.

"What the *hell*?" I snap, pulling away. "If these are my choices, just bring back Baron so he can finish killing me."

"We love you, Marcus."

"Yeah? Well I'm not interested, so stop loving me."

"You have to believe me, Marcus. This is all for you. We really want what's best for you."

"Why do I have to believe you?"

"Because . . . you recognize me. You know me."

A shiver trills up and down my back. But I must not react. I must not let it get to me.

"I don't know you from Adam."

"Yes, you do. And you know there aren't a lot of people like us. You are afraid and alone and aching for an explanation that makes sense."

"And you have that for me?"

"Nope. I have an explanation, all right. But I'm afraid it's not going to make a lot of sense. I'm going to ask for faith."

"I don't believe in faith."

"Fair enough. But I'm going to ask you to stop hiding from what you are seeing. To stop denying what you don't like just because you don't like it. It's time for you to come over."

I wait. Am I giving myself up to my enemies when I open up?

Enemies. There's one right there. Enemies. Do I actually have enemies, and if so, are these them? What the hell am I doing with them? Or is my enemy whatever the hell is hiding behind the attic door? Or are they all one and the same?

"I haven't done anything to you," I say grimly.

Arj hangs his head. He is getting exasperated, but he is not giving up. I wish he would reconsider.

"Of course you haven't, Marcus. Nobody is saying you have. Nobody means you any harm."

"Baron does," I say quickly.

He is about to dispute me, but then "N-no," he stammers. "Okay, Baron does. But that's his problem. Nobody else wishes you any harm. If you will just listen to what I have to tell you."

"Yeah, tell me. . . . You said I was going to meet the head guy tonight. What about that?"

Arj nods. "Sure. You ready?"

"No. I want my dog."

Instantly, the lights bang out again. Then they come

on. We are still standing face-to-face, but we are in a whole different room. It looks like a basement rec room, with a pool table down one end, a Ping-Pong table immediately in front of us, and an old Rock-Ola jukebox in the corner. The walls are corkboard, the floor Astroturf.

"Which one's yours?" Arj asks.

We are surrounded. There are ten cats, Siamese, Persian, marmalade, pacing the periphery of the big room. There is a huge white cockatoo clamping his claws to the edge of the pool table, while a full-bearded pygmy goat licks and nibbles at the felt. An iguana waddles across the tennis table, settling under a light, while a fat Nile monitor looks up at him from flat on the floor. There's a Great Dane the size of a Clydesdale standing next to a woolly sheepdog with a ridiculous ponytail in the middle of its forehead. There is my dog, Chuck, leaning his droopy face so close to the cheek of a sheep that he has to be hitting on her. There are other, smaller creatures here and there, but they do not stop long enough for proper identification, and I think I would just as well have it that way.

And then, there is, around my leg—

"That's a good sign," Arj says, chuckling. "Eartha's snake doesn't like a lot of people, but she seems to have taken a real shine to you."

I cannot even look down at it. My flesh feels like it is rolling off me the way you would remove surgical gloves.

"Get it off," I say stiffly.

"No way," he says. "You think I want fang marks all up and down my arm?"

"Don't play, Arj," I say. The snake is pulling tighter and tighter. The leg is going dead.

"I'm not playing. She's wicked. And she pretty much hates guys."

Still without looking, I reach down and try.

"Sheez." She has done it once more. I raise my hand to see the now familiar neat little holes between my thumb and index finger.

Now I do look down at the snake. I stare at it. I don't know what I am going to do, but something has to happen. I am either going to die of fright or lose my leg.

But of course I don't do anything but stare. Even after she appears to become more interested in my face or neck than my leg. Even when she stretches up, opens those gaping hateful jaws wide, I stare.

Until she just quits. As suddenly and unpredictably as she began. She closes her mouth, uncoils, and slides back down my leg like it's a fireman's pole.

"Really," Arj says. "She really likes you."

"Kind of love/hate, I think."

"Right. So, your friend here, or what?"

"Chuck," I call. He looks over his shoulder at me and makes a new face: I'm busy right now, Dad. "Chuck," I call, and still get no response.

"You should just leave him partying. It's a cool room, huh? Pretty much everybody here is like that, doesn't like to go out without their special little beasts." He smiles. "Seem familiar?"

I don't want to be in this room now. I feel like they are all watching me, the monitor, the frog that the monitor should be eating, the cats and rats and all the others are all looking at me at the same time.

"Let's go," I say.

I follow Arj out of the room, expecting to find the stairs I originally climbed to get here. Instead, this door leads into another room. A plush private bar.

Eartha is sitting there, as are Winston and Marthe. They are drinking ice-blue liquid out of highball glasses. They raise their glasses, saying "Cheers" in my direction.

I keep my distance and attempt to keep my cool.

"So are you this boss then?" I look at Eartha. She shakes her head.

I know it's not her. I know what they want to say. Have for a while. But I want them not to say it. I want to *not* know what they want to say.

"Is it you? Is it you?"

Winston says no. Marthe says no.

"You?" I say to Arj, who is now coming out from around the back of the bar with two more of those big blue specials.

"I already told you, it's not me," he says amiably.

I sigh, slumping onto a tall barstool.

Arj tries to hand me my drink. I push it away. He puts it on the bar in front of me. I notice Eartha, Marthe, and Winston chewing something, then Eartha slides a candy dish my way, filled with what look like bay leaves.

I push it back. "Whatever it is, no."

"You should, Marcus," Marthe says. "We're not going to get anywhere until you relax and open yourself up."

"To what?" I say. I feel like a guy who is lying with his hands tied behind his back and his neck on the block, asking, "So, what's next?"

"To everything," Eartha says, coming to me. "To all things. It is all yours. It is your kingdom." Once more, she kisses me; then I feel her hands running down my face, my neck, my sides, and my hips. I pull away.

"What kingdom, you psychopaths? You people are *so* lost. What do you think, you're special or something? Well you're not. You drink and chew some drug leaves or whatever . . . you learn a bunch of magic tricks, and throw big creepy parties with Daddy's money and you think that makes you *chosen* or whatever. Well guess what? Every high school in America has pods of you freaks, and they don't amount to crap. And I don't know why you decided to pick on me . . . probably you do this to every kid who shows up all weak and alone and new to the town . . . that's what you do, isn't it? That's who you prey on, isn't it? Well you can just screw yourselves this time, all right, 'cause I ain't playing."

I pick up my drink from the bar, not to drink, but for emphasis. I slam it down, creating a small geyser, a rainbow riot of God knows whatever liquids came together in that glass and are now splitting off, into red and yellow and green droplet showers.

I march over to the door and nobody has the guts to try to stop me. I open the door I came in through, stomp out, slam it behind me.

And walk right into the room I just left.

"This really will go better if you have a drink," Arj says.

"Could it possibly go any worse?" I ask.

"Yes," they all say as a chorus.

I walk to the bar, pull up my chair, and slouch in among them. I can't yet get into the intense, eyeball-to-eyeball encounters these folks thrive on, so I look straight ahead, at the long, pink, marble-framed mirror that runs behind the bar. One by one, the members of the Council do the same, until we are all facing each other, or rather, all facing nobody but seeing everybody. Arj, me, Eartha, Marthe, Winston.

I take a gulp of my drink. It is like taking a hard, quick blast on a canister of compressed frozen air. With eucalyptus.

"Is it Mr. Sedaris?" I ask.

Arj shakes his head. "He's just our adviser."

"Is it Baron? Jesus, I hope it's not Baron."

"It's not Baron."

I take a long drink. Eartha's hand is on my back, rubbing. Arj's hand is on my shoulder. It's as if they are telling me I have some vile, incurable disease. Actually, that would be preferable. That would at least have an end in sight.

"Take another sip, Chief," Winston says.

"Don't call me that." I take the sip, though.

"And maybe," says a new voice at the end of the bar, "you might want to chew one of those leaves." I look up to see Mr. Sedaris's face next to Arj's. I decide then that he is right. I might want to chew one of those leaves. Or all of them.

"Hey," he says when I succumb, "don't bogart those leaves." I pass them down.

I hear low, warm, thumping music. I see heads bobbing in the mirror behind me.

I turn around, and they are all here. Rather, I am there. We are all in the great ballroom I first saw through the keyhole downstairs. And they are all looking at me, all raising tall blue glasses to me. All the familiar animals are weaving among the crowd. Chuck is doing very well with the sheep.

"Prince," they say, as if they have been rehearsing this. "Thank you, Prince."

I have to laugh. Just when it is supposed to start making sense to me, they say the most ludicrous thing yet.

"Prince," I scoff, to Arj. "Prince of what?"

"Don't scoff," Arj says solemnly. "We are no longer great, but we are not nothing."

"*We* as in *what*?" I demand.

"We, your people, last of your line. Brink of extinction. We, the last of the line of Cernunnos, god of Celtic forests."

Without my noticing, the entire room has pulled in close around me. This, to me, is a forest. I feel I cannot breathe.

"We have been waiting a long time for you," somebody from the crowd says.

"No, not for me. I don't know who you've been waiting for but it's not me. I'm no Celtic anything. I'm American, and that's all I am. And I'm pretty sure I'm not related to any gods."

"We almost lost faith," another adds.

"We *never* lost faith," Winston says.

"You've apparently lost your hearing," I say.

"We waited, and now we are rewarded," Arj says.

Rewarded. They are rewarded with me. I feel very sorry for their faith. But I cannot help them.

"I can't," I say, and start shoving my way through the crowd. "Chuck," I call, and whistle. He comes trotting between the legs of the people.

Once more, nobody tries to stop me, and I almost let myself believe I am home free.

Until, of course, I get down the hall.

Mr. Sedaris greets me at the front door.

"What?" I snap.

"You can't," he says.

"Yes, I can."

"No, you can't. You can't let a people die, just because you are a coward."

"To hell with the whole bunch of you. I'm not letting anything die, except maybe one Key Club full of deranged drama queens."

"Yes, you are. That room contains every remaining Cern of this generation in this part of the world. There are pods about this same size, scattered through the British Isles, Galicia in Spain, Brittany in France, and Nova Scotia. That is it."

"Fine," I say. If any small piece of it is true, then they have my sympathy. But they do not have my services. "Let one of those people take care of it, then."

He is shaking his head at me. "They are all looking here. You are the one. The line of princes, descended from the seed of Cernunnos himself, leads back several centuries B.C. to the forests of Gaul and beyond—and forward, to modern Western Europe, Port Caledonia, Blackwater . . . and you, Marcus Aurelius. Every Cern in the world knows about you and has been greatly anticipating your emergence. You are our one and only."

"I am not. This is your heritage, maybe, but it means nothing to me."

"Marcus, you need to go back and get a better look at your roots. Somebody's not been telling you the truth."

"I think everybody's not been telling me the truth."

"We need you, Marcus. You are all we have, or we are no more."

I look at him, trying to detect the joke, the playacting, the mean-spirited trick. I detect nothing. I look at Chuck, who refuses to light the tunnel for me.

"I guess you are no more, then," I say, brushing past him.

I am out the door.

I am in the woods.

The Port Caledonia woods. I look all around, and there is no Chuck. I am alone again.

But not. Straight ahead, about thirty feet away and walking steadily toward me, is the man. *The man with the mismatched eyes.*

I jump, or rather *move* myself back inside. Mr. Sedaris is waiting.

I am screaming at him as I point at the door behind me. "All I want to know is, am I hallucinating? Are you freaks in *here* now?" I am pointing, as though I'm holding a gun, suicidally, at my temple.

He is again shaking his head. "Whatever you saw was real, not imagined. That is the thing, Marcus. You have no idea yet, what you can generate, or what you will attract."

I stand, all but at his mercy. I hold my hands out at my sides, begging, "Why me?"

"Because," he whispers, "you are The Progeny. The Son."

"The son of who?"

"The Progeny of the Betrayer Prince."

I am pointing now, right in his face. He blanches, as if in real fear. "You're as whacked as the rest of them, aren't you, you old pervert. Why don't you—"

"Your father was Our Father, Marcus. He was the heir to Cernunnos. He was the Prince of our people, and then he betrayed us, he broke us. You are now rightly the Prince. You were sent to us for this purpose. You were sent to make good. You have a destiny. The line of our god runs directly through you."

"I never knew your *god*, and I never knew my father. And neither did any of you."

"Not personally, no. But I have seen him."

"I don't believe you."

"So tell me, why you are a witch?"

"I never said I was—"

"Are you going to look me in the eyes and say you know of nothing unusual about yourself?"

I would like to, that's for damn sure.

"I . . . all right, I can't say that, no."

"Right. And where do you think you got those powers? Is your mother a witch?"

"Certainly not," I say curtly.

"Right," he says. "And tell me this: how do you feel when you enter the forest?"

It is so unfair, that they know so much about me.

"None of your business, that's how I feel."

"Do you feel power and contentment when you are in the forest? Yes, you do. Do you feel special, unique? Do you feel like a lord, when you are in the forest? Yes . . . you . . . do."

Even as he says it, I am feeling it. My chest is expanding, pounding, my stomach is a cavern of beating wings—hawks, not butterflies.

Yes . . . I . . . do.

"That is because, Marcus, in the forest, you are Lord."

He has tapped something in me, Sedaris has. Some part of me has stopped fighting, and this is no good, no good. I was doing badly enough fighting with my whole being.

I don't want this, though. I don't want to want it.

"That doesn't mean I have to listen to any of this," I say. "Make somebody else Prince. I don't have the stomach for it, and I don't owe anybody anything."

"Yes, you *do*," Arj snaps, slamming the ballroom door behind him. "His sins are your sins."

"I don't believe that. I don't have to believe that."

"You have to, Marcus. We, our people, are one, you

understand, just like I told you from the start. We are a single entity—that is how we have survived through the centuries. And as a single entity, we cannot survive without our head, any more than that dog of yours can survive without his."

I am starting to get the creepy, ominous feeling again.

"Chuck?" I call uncertainly.

"When your father left us, he left us bereft. He left us with the pathetic strands of power you see around here. We do not make proper Obair, we do not reproduce ourselves, we do not, ultimately, survive."

I am weighing my options: none of them very promising. What they call pathetic strands of power are still way more than I can comprehend. Going through doors doesn't seem to get me anywhere. Life as I understand it doesn't even seem to exist anymore.

But I don't want any part of this. I'm sorry, but I don't.

"I'm sorry," I start to tell him. "I wish I could help you people, but I'm just not the—"

"I told you," Baron says, appearing on the stairs.

"Shut up," Arj yells.

"I told you he wasn't it. Why don't you just go on and leave, Marcus. You're no good to anybody. Go on. Screw you." He continues his descent, appearing almost to float his way down.

"Quiet," Mr. Sedaris says.

"No. We'll do fine without this faker. We *deserve* extinction if you're the best we can do."

I don't care. In fact, I'm happy to have somebody, anybody, helping me get out of here.

"You're right, Baron," I say. I open the door to the ballroom to retrieve my dog and leave through that front door, no matter what I find on the other side.

"That's right," Baron adds, laughing. "Run along home. Any Prince who crawled out of that drunk-ass mother of yours can't do anything but pollute us into oblivion anyhow."

There is a sound in my ears like two jets shooting through the room. I turn away from the door and see both Mr. Sedaris and Arj backing away from me. I am doing that thing again, with my arms extending in Baron's direction. He is saying something to me, but I cannot hear him because of the screaming in my ears.

I am so hot it is unbearable. I can actually see my pulse beating in the corners of my eyes. Sweat is pouring down over my brow, down my face and neck. My shirtfront is soaked.

Baron is backing up the stairs. I am seeing him, then I am seeing flashes of somebody else. It is that man again, that face. Then he is gone, and Baron is trying me with the half smile, the outstretched hands. He is pleading, but I am not hearing.

I don't want to move. The man flashes in my head again, and I have a vision of the sweat now turning to blood as it runs down over my face. Something is going to happen, and I do not want it to. I need to be gone. Right here, right now, I know that some part of me is capable of large and brutal, unpredictable, powerful things, and I dread it.

I shut my eyes, only to see the face, the man, the blood . . . Eleanor.

I open my eyes, enraged. I stay planted. This will pass. I don't have to go up there. If I thought I could just hit him, then I could do it. It is beyond me, though, beyond what I control. Beyond what I can even understand, so I cannot predict, cannot allow . . .

Baron backs up and up and up, almost to the top. . . .

Where I appear. Not me myself, as I am still here at the bottom, but me nonetheless.

Baron spins, sees, nearly falls down the stairs until I, or whatever part of me is up there, reach out and catch him.

By his rotten evil tongue.

Baron freezes. There is a pause. The me up there starts down the stairs, dragging Baron down behind him. Baron flails, struggles for balance, tries desperately to keep up, while screaming the whole way like a madman.

When he gets to the bottom of the stairs, the other me comes straight to me. I, like everyone else around, am petrified. His face is cold, unmoved, looking into my eyes while Baron continues shrieking.

I stand, stand, stand, sweating, waiting.

He is impassive, waiting, waiting.

Until finally I feel it. I sense it.

I am to make a decision.

On a life.

"No," I say, desperately. "Jesus, no!"

His expression never changes, the other me. He looks for another instant into me, then adds one last nasty jerking motion as he releases Baron, who falls, crashing like a sack of soup bones, onto the marble floor.

The other me disappears in silence, back up the stairs, back into his blackness.

I back up against the wall as Arj and Mr. Sedaris rush over to Baron. There is a fair bit of blood spilling over his bottom teeth and lip.

"Can you fix it?" Arj asks Mr. Sedaris. Baron keeps screaming and spurting blood.

"I can do *something* with it. I'm not sure how much," Mr. Sedaris says.

People begin spilling out of the ballroom into the hallway. They are gawking and they are gasping.

"Take him," Arj barks. "Take him that way and do it in the kitchen." He gets Baron to his feet, then points a finger into his gaping mouth, at his dead-meat, mutilated tongue. "Guess you better learn to watch this, huh?" he growls at Baron.

Arj gives Baron and Mr. Sedaris a shove, and they stagger off toward the kitchen.

"Everybody go back, go back in," Arj says, waving the party guests back inside. All but the members of the Council of Youngers retreat. The five of us stand in the foyer. I am in shock.

"Did you see that?" I whisper. I am staring at the blood on the floor.

"I did," he says.

I am still struggling to work it out. To come to grips with the thing that was me.

"He's pretty bloody scary," I say.

Arj lets out a respectful small laugh. "He bloody is. You're going to have to learn to control him, Marcus. Do you understand what I'm saying? Do you grasp the depth of this? You *must* learn, because he's not going away. You're going to have to get to know him, quickly."

"Jesus," I say, the hugeness of it beginning to accumulate in my head. There is a flash of light from behind the kitchen door, followed by an extended scream out of Baron and a lot of thrashing and crashing around. Followed by silence. "Jesus . . . oh Jesus."

Mr. Sedaris comes walking down the hall toward us. His clothes are spattered all down the front with blood, and his hands are blackened, as from a fire.

"Well?" Arj asks.

"He'll have a bit of a lisp for a while. He'll be all right. He's out for now."

Out sounds like an excellent idea. "I want to go," I plead. "Can I go now? I mean, without any tricks or spells or confrontations or anything? I just . . . I really need to get away, home, now."

"I guess tonight was kind of a large dose," Winston says, clapping me on the back. I jump. "Sorry," he says, and gives me the last of his drink. I take it.

"May we escort you, Prince?" Eartha says.

"If you don't call me that," I say.

★   ★   ★

The sun is up. It is a typically balmy Carolina morning as we walk along the river. Eartha and Marthe lead, followed by me and Arj, and then Winston and Chuck.

"This is a great dog, " Winston says, throwing a stick into the water for Chuck to fetch. Chuck lets out a little stutter laugh that sounds like "Yeah, right."

The farther we walk, the more businesslike Arj gets. He has an agenda.

"We never told you everything," he says.

"I don't want to know everything," I say.

"You need to know something."

"Whether I want to or not."

"Unfortunately, yes."

Our feet are soaking wet, but nobody seems to notice. We trudge along in step, and I realize that I am surrounded like a heavily guarded criminal, or a head of state. I am cocooned.

I have to say it is not the worst feeling I have ever had, to have a posse of my own. I have never even belonged to a group before, never mind led one.

And I have never before felt so badly that I needed one.

"Okay," I say to Arj, "you tell me I'm supposed to get this . . . thing under control. How do I do that?"

"I don't know."

"What? What do you mean, after all this—"

"This is what I wanted to tell you. There is only one who can help you, Marcus, and therein lies our quest.

You need him. And we need him. A Cern pod in Brittany needs him. And another in the Outer Hebrides needs him."

Everyone stops walking at once. My posse, my cocoon, my coven, pack, my pod, is turned inward, in a circle, around me. Even my dog.

"My father is dead," I say coolly, though I do not feel any kind of cool.

"Like hell he is," Arj says.

...ell and still get no response.

"You should just leave him partying in a cool room hotel. Pretty much everybody here is like that, doesn't like to go out without their special little beasts." He smiled... seemed laughing.

PART
THREE

I wake up screaming, sweating rivers, screaming.

"Jules, Jules, Jules, Jules!"

Then someone is holding me and shushing me, stroking my face.

Jules. It is Jules.

"Jules," I say, and hold her naked body to mine. "God, I'm so sorry, so sorry, I am so sorry."

She doesn't say anything for a few minutes, just holds me, stroking the back of my matted head. Which is just what I need. I don't need words, I don't want words.

"Eartha," she says. "Remember? Eartha."

I let go, lean back, and take in every inch of her. Every inch of her is Jules, nonetheless.

"I forgot," I say dejectedly.

"I wish I were, Marcus. More than anything, I wish I were Jules. I want to be your princess."

I fall back on the pillow. My princess. My destiny. My god.

I sit up quickly again. "My mother. Oh god, does my mother know you're here?"

"I don't think so. I heard her go out a while ago. And last night, well, this morning"—Eartha pauses for a brief giggle—"you didn't even know I was here. Till just now."

I lie back once more with my hands over my face. Clouds are coming in over the muggy Blackwater morning. Smells like rain. Eartha scootches over, lies across me, her cheek and her hand flat to my chest.

I have to ask. "Did we . . . ?"

"We did if you think we did," she says, kissing my nipple, holding her lips there in a smile.

"I can't stand another one of those answers, Eartha, I swear."

"I'm sorry," she says, and goes melancholic. "We did it as much as we can. That's part of . . . the legacy. Try as we might—and make no mistake, try we do—we don't consummate. We love. We entwine. But when it comes to *it*, the experience is like disappearing into a blackness, then coming out the other side. There is no joy, no ecstasy. We pass through physical love without existing in it. It's like having blackouts."

She goes quiet. Kisses my chest once more. The rain begins outside, tapping lightly on the sill of my open window.

"That's why we might seem a little casual about it to you."

"I'm sorry," I say.

She smiles, turns her head to face me directly. "You should be." She is only half joking.

"This is part of what my father is supposed to have caused?"

She nods. "Cern law. Unbreakable. You marry within the tribe."

"And because my father did not . . ."

"That's right. Because he mated with someone outside, a nonwitch, all of us are punished by Cernunnos himself. A great nothingness of conjugal love. And if we try to do what he did, mate outside our species, legend says that the physical pain is beyond all endurance."

Oh yes. Oh yes, this. This, I know. This is where I came in.

It is starting to appear that I have an awesome load to make up for. I have no illusion, in the light of day, that I am going to be up to it.

"That's why, Marcus, you are the youngest Cern left on earth. And the only one of your kind. Regeneration of our people stopped dead, with you, at the moment of your conception."

I did not want words today. This is why I didn't want words today. Everything I hear lately makes things worse, makes them darker and meaner and scarier, and it all keeps leading back to me.

"I think if you tell me any more, Eartha, I might kill myself."

"That's the main thing we cannot let you do. You have to live, to take care of us. You have a preordained assignment, and if you do not meet it, we are finished. Sins of the father. He made us impure, and you are here to repurify the race."

"Why hasn't someone else tried to bring him back in all this time, huh? And how am I even supposed to locate him?"

"Same answer to both questions. Nobody can locate him. But he will locate you."

"Where, when, how?"

"I don't know, I don't know, I don't know." Eartha gets up on her hands and knees, and I am nearly blind, with longing for her, with visions of Jules, with longing for Jules. "But at the end of your journey, I am going to be waiting, to make love with you, with you alone, and for real."

I am fortunate that my heart is only seventeen years old. It would not survive one day with the Cern people at anything less than full strength. It beats so hard at this instant I think it may shoot out of my chest and splatter Eartha, myself, the walls. . . .

"Marcus Aurelius," comes the call from downstairs.

It's my mother.

"It's my *mother*!" I jump out of bed, scramble around for clothes.

I motion silently for Eartha to stay put. She giggles. "And stop that," I say.

I throw on the shirt I wore to the party. It reeks. I throw it off, get a tank top out of the drawer and a pair of soccer shorts off the floor, and beat Eleanor to the door.

I guide her back down the stairs, my arm around her shoulders. "Breakfast?" I ask sweetly.

"At three in the afternoon I don't think they call it breakfast anymore," Eleanor says.

Whatever they call it, Eleanor and I sit down to it. We're both having trouble getting around to business.

"More coffee?" she asks.

I shake my head, stuffing in the last piece of my bacon-and-egg sandwich.

"Really? You look like you could use more coffee."

"Okay, I'll have more coffee."

She pours and takes the opportunity to ease into what she wants to say.

"A person normally has to work at it, to wind up looking like you do. What time did you get home? I never even heard you come in."

"Neither did I," I say. This is not the right tack. Eleanor gives me a very long leash, but if I give her cause to worry, she will worry with the best of them.

"When I said I wanted you to start mixing socially, Marcus, I didn't mean you had to dive right in at the deep end."

I reach out and put my hand over hers. "It's not like that. Okay? Relax."

"All right, then. What is it like?" She leans back in her chair, away from me. She is regarding me with the most suspicious look. Like I am giving off some kind of scent and she is a police dog.

"Where's Chuck?" I ask.

"He's under your chair. The party, Marcus?"

I look under my chair. What do you know.

"It was . . . fun. It was . . . interesting."

"Perhaps I'm being too vague. Is there anyone in your room, Marcus?"

I am still trying to find that corner of my life where I can crawl and hide and find things a little easier. It is not in sight.

"No," I say weakly.

"I see," she says. She has a deeply dubious look on her face. She has somehow caught my trail and won't settle for crap.

I am opening my mouth to say something anyway, when I see Eartha, outside the window behind Eleanor's shoulder. She smiles, she waves. She vanishes.

"There is nobody in my room," I say with conviction. "First, Eleanor, do I lie to you? Mostly, no. And second, how often is anybody in *my* room? Honestly. And if you don't believe me you can just feel free to go right up there and check."

I am sounding pretty well indignant, I figure, when Chuck lets out one of those superior, disapproving dog groans. I kick him.

"Hmm," she says, her tone capturing that limbo I'm in, between being accurate and being believed.

"So how was your night?" I ask, easing us out of the deep water.

She holds for an extra beat, holding me in her stare to let me know she knows there is more. Then she releases me. For now.

"It was lovely," she says, clearly happy to finally have

somebody to share it with. I am pleased to be that somebody. "The entire department is lovely. As far as I can tell, not a bad apple in the bunch, and that is an amazing thing in this field. Now, my position is primarily research, but the possibilities are very broad. I might wind up taking over one section of a course, and Dr. Spence is already talking to me about possibly sitting on some committee things."

"Committee things," I say, nodding. "This is good, yes?"

"Oh yes, well, it may sound dull, and may in fact ... yes, this is all very good. Dr. Spence says he will be watching me closely, taking me under his wing as it were. . . ."

Eleanor is still talking, but my mental train has jumped the tracks. Dr. Spence. Dr. Spence, as in Eartha's father. As in, if I am the only mortal/Cern crossover there is . . .

Dr. Spence, the witch. Is taking my mom under his silver wing.

I feel a chill.

"What . . . Jesus, Marcus, what *did* you do to yourself last night?" Eleanor asks, coming over to feel my head and rub my back. It is pure Eleanor, scolding me with her tone and soothing me with her hands. "Your skin feels like fish scales."

"Sorry," I say.

"What are you apologizing for?"

"Sorry. Habit. I mean, I'm all right. I just . . . you know what it is, I think I just still haven't gotten myself acclimated here yet. I didn't realize how much I had come to rely on my time in the woods in Port Caledonia. I need to get outside more, is what it is. Nightlife . . . not for me, you know?"

"It certainly is not. This is a good lesson for you. Don't get caught up in whatever nonsense is going on with the kids here, Marcus. You be your own man. Make new friends, partake fully of the life around you, but in the end you need to remain you. You have never been a follower. I don't expect you to start now."

She rubs my back the whole time she is along. She, in fact, rubs harder and harder as she goes along. I look up at her.

"You've been waiting to give me that speech."

"Been working on it all day," she says, letting out a gasp of breath that she has also been holding all day.

I stand, feeling more steady already. "Well, it was great. And dead-on. Thanks, Eleanor." I kiss her on the cheek. "I am dying to hear more about Dr. Spence and all later. You'll tell me everything, right?"

"Maybe," she says coyly.

I get a smaller chill, but a chill that's unmistakable.

"And you will tell all as well?"

"Maybe," I say, trying to sound coy myself, but probably sounding more motion-sick. "But right now, I'm going for a long walk in the forest with my faithful companion."

My faithful companion whimpers and stays under the chair.

I pull him out by the collar.

"I'll be a new man when I get back," I say.

"The old one will do just fine," she says.

Come to think of it, that would be fine. Into the woods, locate the old life, the old simple Marcus, and bring him back alive.

"I'll see what I can do," I say, dragging Chuck out the front door.

Chuck continues to be reluctant the whole way. He is not fighting me so much as he is dragging along. I keep turning to him, talking to him, threatening him, without stopping while I do it. I was not joking about my need to get into the woods.

"I'm not in the mood, Chuck, you hear me?"

He hears me fine. His step quickens.

We have to walk briefly through neighborhoods, past corner shops, the post office, the whole movie-set town center, all the opposite of woodland, to get to my woods. When we do reach the edge of the forest, and the scent of pine and turf and dry end-of-summer oak leaf hits me like a bracing slap in the face, I stop and close my eyes.

If there is an *it* for me and Chuck, then this is it—this smell, this feeling. I can tell he is with me on this. He is leaning into the scent now, not pulling back. It is drawing him like it does me.

"Don't worry. Nobody's going to pull you down again."

It may be the forest filling me with strength. But now for the first time I allow myself to embrace my . . . situation, a little bit.

"Nobody's going to screw around with my dog. In my woods."

I cringe almost physically, waiting for something. Waiting for my comeuppance. For a tree to fall on me, a broom to swoop out of the sky, or my dog to burst into flame. Nothing happens. I have gotten away with it.

An Obair. I am The Business.

"Come," I say to Chuck, returning to my real status, "allow the Prince to carry the stinking beast on his back up a tree. What a glorious kingdom it is I rule."

Chuck doesn't laugh, but he does follow me farther in. The whole thing stops being funny to me too in short order. We skulk through the woods with all the seriousness of hunters tracking deer. Every time one of us makes an unusually loud snap underfoot, we freeze. We wait. We start again.

What is it? Are we afraid of spooking our quarry?

Or are we afraid we *are* the quarry and don't want to give ourselves away?

Either way, the forest still doesn't feel completely mine, the way the old one did.

"This is silly," I say and hoist the dog on my back. I have chosen an oak, thicker, taller than the one we adopted in Port Caledonia, and ten times the tree we climbed last time in this very wood. It is a long, long, exhausting shinny, and Chuck must be eating bark on the way up, because he is gaining weight rapidly.

We are probably forty feet off the ground when we sling ourselves over the broad, smooth, muscular arm of a branch. I lie flat on my belly, my chin on my hand on the branch, wiped out with the effort. Chuck remains draped over me like a caveman's bearskin. He is snoring like a sawmill, as if he has done something.

I look out at the view and like what I see. I see as much treetop as anything. Oak and beech and silver maples, punctuated with the arrowheads of a million pines, sliced through with bolts of white birch, here, and here, and here. There is one perfectly oval clearing of meadow a quarter-mile west, and another, more raggedly shaped clearing off to the north. The rain has stopped for now, but the air is thick enough with moisture that you can hold up one finger for seconds and then lick off the sweet, piney dew. The woods are orchestral with the tip-tapping of billions of droplets rolling off leaves, and of hundreds of bird species singing over them.

Everything that has been happening to me, around me, because of me, is for the moment behind me. This is not Port Caledonia, but it is starting to feel like my place.

It is mine. Peace is momentarily mine. For however long, I will take it.

"Don't turn around."

With a gasp, I clutch the tree branch so hard, either it or my ribs will have to break.

The deep, calm voice is right in my ear, where my dog is supposed to be.

"You don't scare me," I say.

"Yes I do."

"No," I say more firmly, "you don't. Nothing scares me anymore."

"That is good. A well-told lie is a fine act of magic.

But it is a lie all the same. I do scare you. And you scare yourself."

He is getting heavier, pinning me harder.

"Go to hell," I say.

He says nothing.

"I'm sick of you people. Where's my dog?"

"You need to stop worrying about your dog. Your dog knows what he's doing. Worry about what needs worrying about."

"And what might need worrying about then?"

"Worry about the truth," he says, whispering ever lower in my ear so that I can hear his tongue making contact with the roof of his mouth. "Worry about knowing. Worry about what you did, about what you might do, and about not knowing. Worry about where you're going, and who is watching. Worry about friends, worry about enemies, worry about finding out. Worry about who is lying to you, and about why. Worry about your back, Marcus. Worry about your head."

It is as if he has taken the events of the journey from Port Caledonia to Blackwater and crystallized the whole thing. Worry about my head? I am way ahead of him.

"Is that all?" I ask wearily.

"No. Worry about Eleanor," he says.

I am startled at the sound of my mother's name. There is a rush of something hot through me, all liquid and speed, spreading from my chest through to the farthest reaches of my fingers and toes. I make the effort. I push up off the branch, trying to get up, to get position on him.

At first, he tries to remain controlled, to hold the balance over me without seeming to try. But I am stronger right now, I can feel it—stronger than I have ever been, and he has to work. I hear him breathing harder, a groan of effort slipping out, as finally with one powerful hand gripping my neck and the other squeezing mercilessly on my kidney, he has me well pinned once again to my branch.

"The spirit is willing," he says, puffing through the words. "But you're not quite The Business yet."

I say nothing. It is all I can do not to wail with the pain. I won't give him that.

"There is a gift waiting for you at home. Go and claim it."

"Go to hell," I say.

"Yes. Well. You will understand better, in time. In the meantime—"

"In the meantime," I cut in, "I think maybe what I should worry about is you."

He breathes deeply, exhales, loosens his grip on me.

"Yes, I suppose, in your position, it would be foolish not to."

There is a pause. Then there is an easing. Then Chuck is again breathing his comforting familiar reek over me.

I straighten up, slide him off my back, then turn around to face him on our branch.

"You're a hell of a watchdog there, Chuck."

It's there on his face. He does know.

If I'm supposed to be the Prince, why does everybody know what I don't?

I turn my back on Chuck and survey the landscape. I am so angry, at I don't know what. "I am going to move something, goddamnit."

I turn and look around. They are vast, these woods.

"They will all be yours," he says.

I whip around again, but there is only Chuck.

I turn, determined to flex whatever magic muscle I might have. I am going to move something. I am going to *control* something. I am not going to be the pincushion for God's voodoo any longer.

"The spirit is willing," he says. A mock.

I don't even look back this time.

"All you survey, it's yours to do with what you wish."

A movement catches my eye, a shimmy, a stirring in a bush twenty yards away.

I lock onto it, burning the bush with my eye. I don't know what I am doing, but I keep on doing it. I stare, I stare, I want it. I want it. I want it to fall under my command.

Chuck starts whimpering.

"Shut up," I say.

I concentrate. I focus. *You are in there, sonofabitch creature, and I want you out.*

It shoots out, a black zigzag that then spikes into a spear, coming at me.

I snag it.

I am holding it by the head, its jaws wide and waiting to strike at me.

I squeeze harder, and harder, and harder.

It is going limp. I squeeze harder.

"I am tired of being watched," I say, my voice deepening. "I am tired of getting bitten. I am tired of being afraid."

I squeeze.

"Don't," he says.

I squeeze harder.

"Don't," he says.

I squeeze until I see some sort of pinkish froth gathering at the corners of its jaws.

"You don't want to do that."

"Don't tell me what I want to do."

His voice deepens. "There is accountability."

I hold on. I can detect no life left in the snake. But I can't yet detect death.

"Even for the Cern Prince. As your power grows, so does your responsibility. Choices are choices, actions have consequences. You will always have to decide. If an act is not you, do not do it. Once done, the act becomes you. Even you do not have the power to make time and undo actions.

"Yet."

He is gone again, and I am staring at the blunt black head of the snake. The jaws are still wide, but they are not rigid. I take my free hand, and move the jaw with one finger. Closed, open, closed, open.

This is not me.

I let go of the head, and hold the entire lifeless thing across my two hands, draped like an old worn belt. I feel a twitch of muscle, then another, as it begins stretching downward, for the branch.

It catches the branch, coils around it, then makes its way for the trunk.

God, I hate snakes. But I want them to die of natural causes.

Behind me, Chuck growls as the snake passes, but leaves it alone.

Together we watch it disappear into the bushes again.

"I don't know," I tell Chuck. "What's the use of this power stuff if this is what it's going to be like? It's like having the keys to the family car but only being allowed to drive it up and down the driveway."

He takes a chew on the back of my shirt, which is pretty bold stuff for Chuck. Then I realize he is not playing. He is tugging and half whimpering, half growling at me at the same time. He is, in fact, pulling me pretty hard.

"You want to go," I say.

He stops pulling. We climb down the tree, and Chuck starts barreling down the path toward home. But this time he's not panicked. Every time I slow down, he stops, turns, and barks at me. All together, this amounts to a week's worth of physical effort for Chuck.

So I have to take him seriously.

I run.

"Eleanor," I call, pushing through the screen door. "Eleanor."

No answer. Chuck barks. No answer to him either.

We go through the business, looking in every corner of the first floor, out on the porch, out over the stream. Then we head to the second floor. No Eleanor in Eleanor's room, or in the bathroom, or . . .

But of course the attic door is wide open. Chuck and I stand there, frozen. The door isn't slamming itself this time, but it is giving off some kind of funky nasty aura.

"Go on, Chuck," I say bravely. I try pushing him from the backside to go up into the attic.

He resists. Does that slinky dog thing where it feels like you're moving them but they're just collapsing their hindquarters.

"Oh, that's enough of this," I say finally. "Whatever it is I'm supposed to see up there . . . I can't just hide forever."

In anger, I shove my coward dog right down to the floor. "You stay, I'll go."

This is fine with Chuck. He stays. I go.

It takes me about forever to make my way down the last ten feet of hallway. It takes even longer for me to make it up the short flight of dimly lighted stairs.

I call out, more to keep myself company than anything else.

"Eleanor?" I say quietly.

"Yes," she answers.

I stumble, retreating back down several steps.

"Marcus," she calls, almost scolding.

I go back up.

"What were you calling me for, if you didn't want to find me?"

"Sorry," I say. "I just didn't figure I would. Find you."

"Well," she says, looking back at the small pile of what she was doing, "you did. I guess it's a day for unanticipated findings."

She is kneeling on the dusty, unfinished floorboards,

picking through an old pine box about the size of a large television. I look at her, then I look away, then I look at her again, then away again.

The place is spooking me to no end. The ceiling is steeply pitched, and there are dark spaces, angles, corners everywhere. It is damp from the rain and from the incessant humidity. I can't stay focused because I can't shake the feeling that something is going to fall on me.

"What are you doing up here?" I ask, catching finally the full worry and sadness on my mother's face. "Eleanor?"

She does not look up all the way, but offers me an angle on her face, caught by the single bare lightbulb. She cannot pull her eyes away from the box.

"The door was open. I thought I heard you up here. I know I heard the doors. I cannot understand. . . ."

I wait for more, for explanation. I wait in vain.

"You don't understand, Eleanor," I say. "I don't either. Can you tell me . . . better, let's go downstairs, and you can—"

"How this stuff got here. I didn't move this box here. You didn't move this box here?"

She is too distressed for this to be any old regular question. She looks up at me now, a sort of pleading in her eyes.

I shudder.

"So," I say, "it was here when we got here. It was left by the last people who lived here. Right?"

She stares down into the box. Shakes her head.

"What's in there, Eleanor?" I squat down on my haunches, like I'm going to look into the box. But I don't inch up any closer.

She is quiet.

Breath is on my neck.

I jump.

"Chuck," I yelp, straightening back up. "Jesus."

Eleanor stays focused.

"It's . . . your father's old black magic . . . *bullshit,"* she snaps. It is meant to be a brave go-to-hell. She sounds scared.

"My whose . . . what?" I ask, walking toward her, and it.

She slams the lid shut, and looks at me sternly.

"We have to talk," Eleanor says.

"Yeah, we do," I say.

We are sitting at the kitchen table. Between us there is a carafe of my mother's homemade sangria, two glasses, a horned helmet, a pewter ring, a gold choker, and a cauldron.

"How could you forget a thing like this?" I ask her as I finger the wildly intricate scenes molded into the bronze sides of the bowl.

"With a lot of effort, that's how."

"But why?" I ask. I can't look at her as she speaks, because I can't take my eyes off the stuff. The helmet is a bit primitive, but that makes it all the more fascinating. It's a sort of dirty bronze, but almost looks like it could be petrified leather, with a mountain etched in the front surrounded by loads of trees and overseen by multiple suns or planets. There is a sort of stitching pattern zigging through it all, and the two fat horns sprouting from the top are of slightly differing sizes.

I put the helmet on.

Eleanor swipes it off.

"Not," she says.

"Are you going to tell me what the problem is?" I can pretty well tell what the problem is. What I want specifically to know is what *her* problem is.

She takes a good long gulp. "The *problem*, young man, is this stupid witch bullshit."

"Um, do you have to keep calling it that?"

"Yes, I do!" she barks.

"Okay," I say. "Go on."

Eleanor picks up the cauldron and turns it around and around in her hands. As if she is viewing old family videos in the scenes depicted in the panels of forests full of griffins and snakes, bulls, boars and giant stags. Each panel is dominated by some big-headed character in a helmet, some with horns, others with snaky embroidered Celtic designs banding their foreheads.

"Crap," she snaps, like she is speaking directly to one or more of the heads. "All of it, utter crap." She bangs the cauldron back down on the table, picks up her wineglass. "Your *father*," she spits, "drove me insane with this nonsense."

"Well, if it's nonsense . . . ," I begin.

"It *is* nonsense." She is taking this awfully personally.

"Then what's the big deal?" I ask. Again, knowing what the big deal is, but wanting to hear her version.

"It is what tore us apart," she says, suddenly twenty fathoms lower than she was. She stares into the bowl.

This would be a good time to not be pressing for details, judging from Eleanor's twisted features. I so wish I could let it alone.

"I thought death was what tore you apart. You never told me you split up, Eleanor."

"No," she says, "I didn't."

"You told me he was dead."

"Yes, I did."

"Well, is he dead?"

I think that if she could crawl into that cauldron right now and dissolve, she would, no matter how much she hates the bullshit.

"I would be very surprised, Marcus, if he were not dead."

Neither one of us is particularly convinced by that answer. But I am not prepared to provoke her any further right now.

"Why didn't you tell me any of this before?"

"I didn't want to upset you."

I can't let this one go.

"Eleanor?" I say firmly.

She refills both our glasses. "What do you think?" she asks. "Needs a little more triple sec and a splash more tequila, I'd say."

I pick up the choker.

"His *torque*," she says bitterly.

"Yeah?" I ask. It is deadly cool, a twisted gold tube an inch in diameter, with two fists meeting in the center where there is a gap. There is a hinge at the back, and I open it, clamp it shut around my neck.

Eleanor shuts her eyes, shudders.

I take advantage of the moment and slip the ring on my middle finger. It is a starkly gorgeous thing, heavy weathered bone carved into the shape of a stag horn, knotted and twisted into itself, around itself, and me. It is a little loose, but it feels right, there on my hand.

"I wish you would just leave it alone, Marcus," she says sadly, weakly. She could certainly put up more fight than this. "I mean, it all belongs to you, I suppose, but—"

"Have you been keeping it all this time?" I am modeling the stuff now. I cannot help it. Creepy as it may sound, I feel a power and a ghoulish thrill coming over me as I turn this way and that, feel the stippled scratch of the gold at my throat, feel the heft of the ring.

"I haven't seen any of it since the day he left," she says. "I thought it all went with him."

This, to me, is not shocking. Not after all I have been seeing. But to Eleanor, feeling the way she feels, this cannot make sense. Eleanor likes sense, and she makes sense.

Anthropologist Eleanor. Making sense is her life, and she has devoted herself to it.

"So do you have a theory?" I probe cautiously.

I count on Eleanor. She is and always has been keeper of the Sense, as far as I know. Her reason is my reason, and if I am going to return to any form of reason now, it is she who will have to bring me to it.

"Eleanor?" I ask.

I watch the twitching of her eyes and facial muscles like I'm watching the blips and bleeps of a computer, as she tries to come to logic.

She takes a deep drink.

So do I.

"No, I don't," she says flatly. "Obviously *somebody* put it here. Either whoever was living here before us, or somebody who got up here in the short time between the previous occupant and us. I will ask Dr. Spence about the previous residents and who might have had access. When I see him tonight."

I gulp. Dr. Spence? Seeing Dr. Spence tonight?

The voice is behind me again, distantly. "Worry about Eleanor," it says.

I turn, and only Chuck is there. His ears are way flat to his head, and his eyes watery.

I turn back to Eleanor, who is looking brighter. She has fought it off for the time being, filed it away where it cannot hurt her.

"Oh," she says, smiling a cracky smile, "I almost forgot. Jules called while you were out."

Jules.

Jules.

I no longer even know what meaning the name has. Love. Nightmare. *Lovenightmare.* I go simultaneously numb and sweaty at the sound of it.

Jules called. Test? Joke? Sangria-fueled psychosis? Whose psychosis, Eleanor's or mine, or some poetic symbiotic mutual dissolve because we just can't take any more of whatever it is we are taking?

"I'd think you'd be more excited than that," she says dryly.

"Sorry," I say, trying to snap back. "Jules, my god. Jules? Are you certain it was Jules?"

"I know Jules, Marcus."

"I know you do, but—"

I have to cut myself off. Which of the various *but*s would I dare go into?

She gives me a look, then goes on. "Says she misses you. And she wants to see you."

It's all falling away quickly, all the spooky business, all the might have's and the surreal head-splitting fear of it all.

Jules.

"She wants to see me," I say, my voice half choked. I can't fight a smile, even if every sensible impulse tells me to duck and cover.

"She does," Eleanor says, reflecting that same smile. "And she says Doone has been asking for you too. Who is Doone? Marcus? Marcus, what is it? Come back here—"

"I have to lie down," I call to her.

I spend the balance of the day on the couch. Running Jules's phone number through my head. *522-1396 . . . 522-1396 . . . 522-1396 . . .*

But the numbers don't leave my head, as my body doesn't leave the couch. The call never gets made. Fear wins again.

"Call her, will you?" Eleanor says during one of her few forays downstairs. She has been preparing for her evening. With Spence. She looks good; long slim skirt, silk blouse. Too, too good.

"What are you up to, really?" I ask.

"Getting a life, Marcus," she says.

I snort.

"Don't snort. Life is good. You should remember that. *Call* her, for godsake."

"It's . . . complicated, Eleanor."

"Try me."

"Don't think so, no."

"Come on, Marcus, I've got some experience with these things, you know. I'm sure I can be helpful."

Not likely, I'm thinking, considering that at worst I'm a murderer or at least certifiably insane, and at best, I am my mother's darkest fear come to life. Come *back* to life. But I know she's not going to just let go.

"Fine," I say, "I'll cough it up if you do. Tell me all about him."

She pauses, walks through the room, into the kitchen, clinks around some silverware, glasses, ice. Comes back.

"Him?"

She knows.

"My dad. The whole gory story, Eleanor. You tell, I tell."

She regards me, one hand on hip, the other to her lips.

"Fair enough," she says. "Keep your secret."

Chuck and I see her to the door.

"You're really going," I say. "On a date. With Dr. Spence."

"I'm really going, yes, Marcus. But I wouldn't call it a date, exactly." She giggles nervously at that.

I fail to see the humor.

Dr. Spence pulls up in his plum-colored vintage Mercedes, waves at me, and gives the horn a little toot. It sounds slowed down and warped, like the bleating of a wounded goat.

Eleanor gives me a kiss on the cheek and tells me, "Don't wait up."

"The hell I won't," I say.

She is kidding. I am not.

As I stand in the doorway watching them drive off, Chuck bumps up hard against my leg. I look down to find him looking uneasy and soupy-eyed, not unlike the way he does during a thunderstorm, just before he bolts for the bathtub. But the skies are clear, and the breeze is soothing.

I ignore his look and head out to the porch to watch the stream flow. It has become, more than anything else, my refuge. I know that it isn't bringing me the bad stuff. It doesn't stop for me, is the thing I appreciate most. It moves right on past, without challenging me or spooking me, without acknowledging or even noticing me at all. Just like the whole rest of the world used to do.

The stream moves downriver. Ceaselessly. Like a stream is supposed to do.

If everybody and everything would just do that, do what they were supposed to do instead of funky flying and speaking and materializing and spooking in ways that I don't understand . . . well, that is about all I would ask out of life.

I sit for maybe a half hour, appreciating the water's fairness. I close my eyes, and the babbling makes the only sense I know. Sweet babble.

522-1396.

I open my eyes.

522-1396.

It's in my head.

That's right. It is in your head.

But that is not *my* inner voice.

No, young Prince, it isn't.

I stand up, and start pacing, pacing the porch. I try to refocus on the cool babbling of the water.

It grows fainter.

You were supposed to watch out for Eleanor. You were supposed to watch out for Eleanor. What did you do?

"Chuck?" I call. "Chuck?"

Why didn't you call her back, Marcus Aurelius?

"What was I supposed to do? She doesn't do what I tell her to do . . . Chuck?"

It is as if the water has stopped moving. The stream is dark, but I still should be able to see the glints of baby whitewater. There is none, and the stone silence is oppressive.

You are supposed to be the Prince, assuming the throne—

"I don't want any goddamn throne. Get out of my goddamn head."

Why did you let her go with him, Marcus? He is not a good man. Why did you let her go with a bad man? You are supposed to be taking control.

"How do I know? How do I know anything? Maybe he's the good man. Maybe you are the bad man."

I am squeezing my own temples now, as if to squeeze out the voice and whatever is attached to it.

"Get the hell out of my *head*!" I scream. "Coward. Sneaky, shadowy spook."

Silence.

The stream flows, my dog returns, the breeze strokes my face, and all is like it was.

Silence.

I can no longer trust it.

522-1396.

This time it is, as far as I can tell, my own inner voice.

Leave me alone anyway, inner voice.

522-1396.

I don't want to call. I don't want to hear Jules's mother tell me how I mauled her daughter and destroyed everybody's life. I don't want to hear Jules herself tell me that no such thing ever happened, and that she is sad to hear that I have lost my mind. I don't want to hear that the police want to talk to me.

522-1396.

I go to the phone. Sweating, my own heartbeat now drowning out the rushing water and everything else, I punch five and two and two and onethreeninesix.

Rings. Rings again and again and again and no way am I leaving any message on this machine and so, *come on*, machine, pick up, pick up, pick up—

"Hello?"

I couldn't speak if I wanted to. I don't want to.

"Hello? Hello?"

It is Jules.

Jules's voice. I dialed Jules's number, and Jules answered.

I stand there briefly, stunned into paralysis. I have to stop this. I have to stop being so surprised by everything.

By anything.

Jules is alive. In Port Caledonia.

So what the hell happened in the first place?

Everything I've felt up until this point—fear, guilt,

fear, loneliness, confusion, and fear—is swept away now on a wave of rage as everything that has happened from Doone's party onward flashes before me. I drop the receiver back onto its hook.

"Who the *hell* is responsible?" I scream into the empty house.

"Chuck!" I call. I whistle. No answer.

I tear around the house. I go to the second-floor bedrooms. I go to the bathroom.

"I can't have you chicken on me now, Chuck," I say as I drag him out of the bathtub. "We're hitting the road. We're going home, boy."

I dash to my room, throw a few things into my gym bag, then go to Eleanor's room, grab the keys to the truck, and scrawl a note on one of her hundreds of little yellow sticky note pads.

Don't worry. I'll call you.

I stick the note to her computer screen and leave.

I am running as I bang through the screen door. I throw my bag in the back and my dog in the front. I slam the door and gun the engine.

I wait before putting the truck in gear. When I do that, this will become for real, and I will see it through.

I close my eyes, rest my forehead on the steering wheel, and listen to the engine strain.

Chuck licks my hand.

"Nice ring," she says.

I open my eyes slowly and regard her. It is Eartha, standing next to the driver's-side window. Of course it is

Eartha. I am not even surprised, and I congratulate myself for it.

"Yeah," I say, looking the ring over from all angles. It looks whiter and feels heavier than before. More like live bone than old carved antler. I don't even remember taking it away from the kitchen table.

And it fits me better than it did. It's hugging my finger like a vine.

"What brings you here?" I say, sighing.

"Ah, well, with your mom and my dad getting all heavy over there—"

I hold up my hands to stop her.

"Sorry," she says. "So, going for a little trip?"

"I am."

"Want some company?"

I lean toward her and speak through gritted teeth. "It hardly matters what I *want*, does it?"

"On the contrary, Marcus, *all* that matters is what you want."

I take a deep breath, count to ten . . . almost.

"Get away from my truck," I snap.

"Okay," Eartha says brightly. She steps back.

And becomes even more Jules in the half-light of the street.

"See, we only want what you want. When you calm down, you will realize that. But listen to me, Marcus. When you meet up with him . . ."

I turn quickly away from her, and grip the wheel as if I have to pay close attention to the road ahead.

"When you meet up with him, be very careful. And

keep your wits. Don't believe everything you hear. Legend has it the Prince of the forest can be very shady—"

"Funny, I seem to be hearing a lot lately, about not believing everything I hear."

She backs a couple of steps away from the car. "Right. Believe yourself, is all you can do."

I let out a hard, nasty laugh and jam the truck into gear. "If I could do that, you all wouldn't be able to screw with me like you do."

"Just remember," she says, as I start rolling out, "that he left us . . . but he also left you, and he left your mother—"

I send rocks and dirt flying as I peel out.

Fury propels me the first couple of hours of the trip. It is only after we have driven that long that I realize how tired I am, and that getting mad and fired up has made me more sluggish than before.

I find myself blinking a lot. Then I find the blinks getting more lengthy, to the point where I have to force my eyelids open and shake my head madly to stay alert.

"Talk to me, will you, Chuck?" I say, which is fairly chancy, the way things have been going. If he does talk to me, I might ask him to take over the driving.

He doesn't talk.

My eyes close.

Jules appears. It is as if I am seeing her on a television screen in close-up. She is addressing the camera as if it is a person, like a soap opera love scene.

She smiles at me, that Jules smile, and I am melted. I

am hers. I have to say that even if I do find her at the heart of this whole cruel horrible scheme, I don't know if I can turn on her, the way I should.

I will turn on somebody, that much is sure.

Jules's face disappears.

I snap to consciousness. I am driving with two wheels in the breakdown lane and two bumping along on the soft shoulder until I jerk the wheel and the truck back onto the road.

I have never been so enraged. I put the pedal down and bear down on Port Caledonia so hard I will shoot through it like a rocket when I get there.

Chuck is whimpering.

"Shut up," I say. "I'll tell you this, Chuck, if I have *any* of the powers these people tell me I have, then somebody is going to pay big-time for this. Somebody is gonna *pay*."

Chuck whimpers more loudly.

"Stop it," I say.

I fixate on the ring on my finger on the wheel.

I can see the lights of Port Caledonia.

I am near tears, but I am nowhere near an explanation for them. Fifty thousand thoughts slalom the slopes of my mind, and none of them give me any comfort. I am unsettled and unsorted, and I am going to get my hands around the neck of this monster and squeeze until there is not a scintilla of life left.

I am going ninety-five miles per hour when I hit the bridge.

And the misty morning fog.

I can't see ten feet in front of the hood. Then suddenly, burning through like a foglight, there is the image. Of Doone Howe. In the middle of my lane, staring straight and cold into me. Chuck is howling, and I am kicking the brake pedal over and over as I swerve madly. I see the lights and hear the foghorn of an oncoming truck and try to swerve back again.

I spin, once, twice. It is like being on the tilt-a-whirl at the carnival, only blind. I grit my teeth, scream, wait for the thump of the bridge abutment.

But it doesn't come. Next thing I see is open milky sky, then the water rushing up toward me. I am weightless, and now I'm choking back vomit.

We hit the water with the force and the noise of a jet engine.

And then, the silence.

We are sinking down, down into the water. My head is pounding so hard I feel like I have been hit with a tire iron. I look over at Chuck, who lies on the floor of the cab, curled in a tight ball as if he's just lying in front of the fire.

We land on the bottom with a thump.

I am panicking. I try to move and am trapped by the belt. I undo it and start pounding the door. I can't open it, and the truck is already filling with water coming in through Chuck's open window.

Chuck has floated up, and is now sort of lying, grotesquely, on the top of the water, at my shoulder's height.

I grab him, shake him. His eyes are open, but he is not really responding.

I grab him mightily by the balls, and hear him yowl, then I shove him out the window and up.

I climb out right behind him.

But I don't make it. My foot is caught. I yank and yank, but it won't come free until I turn and unhook the seat-belt buckle from my boot.

I am just making my way out of the cab, when I bump.

Into Jules.

I hear myself scream under the water, then scream again, as I try to swim backward. She is hideously bloated, blue-green and goggle-eyed, floating there twenty feet from the bottom, dressed in the flowing skirt and blouse that she wore at Doone's party.

I can feel myself beginning to suffocate, as I scream out of control, swallow water, thrash around in every direction other than the surface. My chest is cracking with pain, about to collapse on me totally.

I fade completely into black.

"You are a lucky guy," I hear.

I am listening, but I can't yet open my eyes. I can smell, though, and this is definitely a hospital.

"Cabdriver arrived just as your dog was hauling you up on the bank. That's an exceptional animal you have there."

I know this voice.

I open my eyes slowly. It takes a few seconds to focus

on him even though he is right there, sitting on the side of the bed.

But focus I do. I also know the face. By now, I should know this face and these mismatched eyes.

"Where is my dog?" I ask, trying not to sound too alarmed.

"He's fine," the man says. "One of the nurses took him home for the time being, so he's well cared for."

I stare at the man. He has the white coat, the stethoscope, the clipboard. But no way. No, no way.

He is holding my hand. He is fingering the ring.

"How are you, Marcus?" he says gently.

I don't answer.

He starts feeling my bones, my hands, my arms, my face, my skull.

"She really is dead, isn't she," I say. I have the sensation again, same as when I approached the bridge. I feel like crying, but I can't quite manage it.

It is as if he hasn't heard me. "I think you are okay. You have some bruises, some shock, a little water in your lungs . . . but yes, you are okay."

"No," I say. "I'm not."

His turn to stare.

But his stare is another thing entirely.

As if his beacon eyes have a lunar pull, his glare draws from my eyes the tears that would not otherwise come.

"Is there anything you want to tell me, Marcus Aurelius?" he asks.

I think about it all. I think about watery Jules. I think

about riding my bike in circles and circles six hundred times and all the falls and all the get-back-ups by myself. I think about Eleanor and wine. I think about Jules's blood and hair in my fingers and snakes and moving things, and phone calls and nightmares and forests and tongues and lonely lonely lonely.

I think it all, while he draws the last bits of tears out of me with his lunar eyes.

"No," I say. "Nothing."

He holds me with that stare, waiting, extracting more.

"You aren't a doctor."

"No. But I am here to take care of you. Do you know why *you* are here?" he asks.

"I'm here because I crashed the truck."

He shakes his head, and rubs my arm softly. I let him.

"No, son," he says sadly, as if this is a terrible sad bed-side confession that we both have to bear.

"You're here to kill me, son."

Something terrible has awakened in Marcus . . .

He has power now.
Power he never dreamed of.
Power he can't control.

Marcus' father says he can help him.
Keep him from hurting anyone else.
Like the way he hurt Jules.

BUT WHO CAN HE TRUST?

The man who claims to be the father he never knew?
Or the mysterious coven that wants his power?

CAN HE EVEN TRUST HIMSELF?

Read book two
of the Witch Boy trilogy . . .

Dark Prince
by Russell Moon

Coming in September 2002